Fractured
And
Alone

Loraine Clinton Phillips

Published by Lake Crafts

Fractured and Alone

Copyright © 2023 by Loraine Phillips

This is a work of fiction. Names, characters, events, and most places are a product of the author's imagination or are used fictitiously.

Printed in United States

For permissions contact: author.lphillips@gmail.com

ISBN: 979-8-9903942-0-9

To my husband, Greg,

who encouraged and supported me

through this process.

Thank you for giving me the time and space to write.

Table of Contents

Chapter 1
Unforeseen Events

Bedtime was always a challenge, but tonight it was particularly difficult. More so than any other time Eleanor could remember. Tonight, Madison dug her heals in for the match. Volleying back and forth from reasoning to stomping feet, from pleading to whining, from reversed psychology to yelling, and finally from sternness to crying. It seemed to be a tied game and Eleanor was about to break the tie with a play she rarely used.

She took a deep breath before serving the final volley. "Madison, the game is over. You will stay in the house tomorrow instead of going outside to play with your friends. You will also help clean before your parents return. I love you, honey, but there are consequences for your actions."

Without speaking a word, Madison slowly walked up to her gramma. A foreboding darkness encompassed her as she looked her gramma straight in the eyes and raised her hand with one swift, deliberate move. She stopped, slowly lowering her arm. She wasn't quite able to go as far as her chat room friends suggested. Except for the steely glare, her body was without emotion. For the first time, she loudly spoke, "I hate you." She gave her gramma a warning glance before walking victoriously to her room and slamming the door with a force Eleanor had never before witnessed.

Madison allowed jealousy to take over her mind and heart. Her grandparents, especially her gramma, was spending too much time with her mom. Thankfully she found a new group of friends that understood completely and encouraged her to take action before it was too late. She started spending more and more time in the chat room.

These are my true friends, the ones who get me and the ones who stand with me. They believe me. They give me ways to end this interference.

A quiet voice inside told Madison what she was doing was wrong. She ignored the voice and instead went into the chat room where they applauded what she did. It felt good to please her new friends. Friends she had never met, but friends who were always ready to listen and give her advice. Advice she trusted and believed.

Eleanor stood frozen, touching her face to stop the tears streaming down. Her chest began to constrict and muscles started to become tight, while a sharp pain pierced her lungs, as if she had been running during a cold February morning. She walked slowly to the kitchen for a cold glass of water, hoping to squelch the blazing fire in her heart. She and Logan loved their granddaughter. Watching her grow was a special treasure for them, and one they didn't take for granted.

She had been so happy when David and Ellery asked her to stay with Madison while they were at a dental conference. Madison would turn twelve in September. She was tall for her age with long dark hair and big beautiful brown eyes, like her mom. Her deep-set dimples appeared every time she smiled. She shared her parents love and ability for sports.

Ellery and David desperately wanted children, but with miscarriage after miscarriage, it seemed that was never going to happen. Madison was the miracle baby. Ellery stopped teaching to care for her full time. When Madison started school, Ellery went to work at David's office.

Sitting at the kitchen island, Eleanor replayed what had just taken place. *Did this really happen or is it a bad dream? She often gives me a rough time about certain things, but we always work it out and never with unkind words. She said, I hate you, but she can't mean it? The words were bad enough to hear, but her cold, hateful, and defiant look felt like a demolition team had just leveled my heart. Logan will know what to do. But, I have to be careful not to upset him.* Logan was her rock with his clear head and sound advice. He saw the world in a very practical, yet compassionate way.

Eleanor wasn't sure how to handle this. She was glad Ellery and David would be back tomorrow. *Do I tell them what happened? They may not believe me and decide to drag Logan into it. Maybe Madison was just having a bad day or testing the waters to see how far she can go with me. Whatever it is, I'm sure it's over and hopefully she'll apologize in the morning.*

Eleanor made her way to the bedroom, pausing by Madison's door to make sure she was still in her room. No matter how long she prayed, she couldn't seem to relax and leave it with God. Tossing and turning all night she hoped things would be better in the morning.

Madison finally came downstairs for breakfast with emboldened confidence. She won in upsetting Gramma and it wouldn't be long before she could throw the final strike.

"Good morning, honey. Do you want pancakes or cereal?" Eleanor managed to ask.

The glare was the same as last night; cold as steel and empty. "Don't talk to me."

Eleanor shivered as the temperature dropped to forty

below. Ignoring her words and the ice forming around the room, she tried to sound unnerved. "Madison, Were you upset about something last night? I'm sure you didn't mean to say those words. Why don't we talk about it, and put it in the past. This will be between you and I."

"I wasn't upset at all. For your information, I meant those words." Madison's confidence grew as she restated the words from last night. "I hate you."

"I'm sorry you still feel that way. I won't pretend that it doesn't hurt to hear you say those words." Eleanor had to ask one question, "Do you hate Grampa too?"

"No. Just you." I'll be in my room. Don't bother me." Leaving the kitchen, she flashed a self-satisfied smile. The anger felt good.

Shoulders hunched and trembling, Eleanor laid her head on the kitchen table. When the trembling began to subside, she slowly raised her head and wiped the tears from her face. Claiming back her composure, she began to ready the house for her daughter's return. She decided not to say anything to them about the scene between she and Madison until she first talked to Logan. She needed his wisdom and perspective on this. She hoped it would all blow over.

Ellery and David returned right on schedule. Upon seeing them, Eleanor changed her mind about informing them of the events that had played out.

"Welcome home." Eleanor greeted her daughter and son-in-law.

"Hi, Mom. How did it go?" Ellery asked.

"Well, last night…" but before she could tell them, Madison came running down the stairs, all smiles and full of life.

"Mom! Dad! I'm so glad you're back."

"Hey, kiddo. We missed you a lot." David hugged his daughter tightly.

Eleanor stood there in silence, fighting the panic rising in her already tightened body. Her feet were frozen in place and her mouth dry while wondering what her granddaughter would say.

"Did you have a good time with Gramma?" Her mother asked.

Madison's rehearsed response came out with unbelievable ease. "Gramma and I had a great time," said Madison. "We watched TV, went for a walk and then made sure the house was clean for you."

David laughed. "You see, Ellery, I told you Madison would love the time with Gramma. We could have stayed away longer,"

"Yes, you could have." Madison piped up. "Gramma and I are a team. Aren't we Gramma?"

Eleanor stood there perplexed while struggling to keep

her eyes from the flood of tears begging to be released. All the blood in her face had found somewhere else to be and she prayed it would soon make a return trip before anyone noticed. She was glad everyone's attention was on Madison but it only gave her seconds to try and calm her rattled mind. "Yes. Madison is right. …We are a team." Eleanor wasn't sure how she managed to get the words out as she battled with her emotions. She prayed they couldn't see her forced smile.

"Well, I should let you get settled and spend time with your lovely daughter. I must get back to Logan. I'm sure he is ready for a meal he doesn't have to prepare." Eleanor was glad she thought ahead to put her things in the car that morning, as she put on her coat and headed for the door.

Ellery gave her a big hug. "Thank you, mom. I wish you didn't have to rush off, but I'm so glad that you and Madison had a good time."

Madison hugged and kissed her gramma. "Thank you, Gramma. I'm going to miss you." Then, so only her gramma could hear, "You know, I really do hate you."

Eleanor grabbed for the doorknob, afraid she would fall after the verbal slap to her heart. Somehow, she opened the door and made it to the car before feeling completely weak. She made it a few blocks before pulling over. Resting her head on the steering wheel, she wept.

Closing the door, Eleanor found Logan asleep in his usual place, watching the latest game. Her face softened as she watched him. He was tall and very handsome, with sandy blond hair that had silver streaks running through it. She thought about his gentle face and godly heart, then winced at burdening him with what happened.

With a quiet sigh, she left the room to put her things away. Logan had been a three-sport athlete in high school and went on to play baseball in college. He was strong, and until recently, very much in shape for a man in his early sixties. *I tell Ellery to always hold on to the memories. Memories are a gift to press close to your heart, and now, it is my turn to savor the memories.*

Returning to the family room, she was happy to see Logan awake and alert, she bent down and gave him a kiss on the cheek. "Hi sweetheart. I'm home. How have you been?"

"Better now that you are here. I did just fine fending for myself, but I am awfully tired of being alone."

"Well, I'm here and not planning on leaving anytime soon. Are you hungry or did you eat lunch already?"

"I am starving! I fell asleep before making lunch. Sure could use one of your famous sandwiches." Logan said, giving that little boy look he did so well.

Eleanor chuckled. "Give me ten minutes."

"Sounds wonderful. Almost as wonderful as having you home." Logan squeezed his wife's hand.

They ate in almost complete silence, except for the latest game playing in the background. Logan noticed his wife was mulling something over and sat waiting for her to be ready to share.

"Logan. Something happened with Madison that has me confused and a little hurt. I can't seem to figure it out, but maybe you can."

Logan moved closer to his wife. "I am all ears. "

"I'm sure it's nothing more than Madison getting closer to her teenage years. She wants to test the waters, be independent, and push the limits. I don't want you to get upset, but you need to know." Looking at Logan she caught the concerned look on his face. She prayed it wouldn't be too much for him.

"The first two days Madison was herself. We talked, played a few board games, and ordered pizza. All the typical things we do together. Each day she became quieter and had less and less patience with me. Typical for her age, right? Then, last night she carried on about not wanting to go to bed."

Logan took her hand. "Did something else happen? Because what you have said so far isn't out of the ordinary for her."

His gentle touch caused the dam to break and spill onto her face as she started to relay the events of her final night with Madison. "I wasn't going to tell Ellery and David, but I changed my mind when they walked in the house. Before I could talk to them, Madison came in happy and told them we had a great time together. I know I should have said something, but I just stood there, afraid."

Logan closed his eyes and prayed for Eleanor and for Madison. His heart was breaking for his dear wife and what she was feeling. He loved his granddaughter, but couldn't imagine her acting in such an extreme manner. He gently held his beloved and whispered how much he loved her.

The two of them sat in silence for a while, holding each other. Logan sensed she was ready for him to speak. "We need to pray about this, my dear. Only God knows the heart of our granddaughter. We can only reach out in love, no matter what she may say or do."

"Praying is the easy part." Eleanor said, "Not showing the hurt and disappointment isn't. You aren't the one she hates. It's me and only me. I don't know why or what I've done. I replayed the last several years, every event, every visit, every conversation, and I can't figure out the why."

Logan softly responded. "My dear Eleanor. I realize you wanted to keep this to yourself because of my health, but it would have been worse on me not knowing. I pray, that before my days are gone, you and Madison will share that special relationship once more."

"Do you think I should have told them? Should I tell David and Ellery now or wait and see? I don't want to make matters worse."

"There are pros and cons to this. Why don't we pray on it and see if things get back to normal in the next week or so? If they do, then this will be between you and Madison. If after a few weeks it continues, we will sit down with Ellery and David. Sound good?"

Eleanor nodded. "I know they should know about Madison's behavior when they were out of town, but I don't want to cause more problems, especially if it only happened that one time." She had to protect Logan at all costs. She would not let any conflict between her and Madison upset him. The last thing Logan needed was a family explosion. His time remaining must be filled with love and laughter; not sorrow and tension.

Logan knew his wife was protecting him, and even though it warmed his heart, he questioned whether it was the right thing to do. He knew God had to work in her heart and give her peace about it. He led them in prayer, asking God to touch Madison's heart and ease the pain in theirs.

Eleanor covered her sleeping Logan with an afghan and settled into her favorite chair. She picked up her knitting. It wasn't long before the knitting needles dropped to her lap and her eyes closed. Sleep had finally taken over.

For the next few weeks Eleanor and Logan had dinner at Ellery's and attended a few social events where their granddaughter was present. Each time, Madison was the perfect granddaughter; an outstanding actress, fooling everyone that observed her performance. So much so, that Eleanor received compliments from her friends.

They so envied how close she was to her granddaughter, and Madison's devotion to her. People only saw the so-called warm hugs and kisses on the cheek. They saw the smiles of a devoted granddaughter. But what they missed were the whispers 'I hate you'.

Madison had no remorse for what she did, nor for what she was doing. She believed the change in her was for the best and everyone would benefit from what she was doing, especially her. For Eleanor, her role in her granddaughter's performances were getting easier to play. She was getting better at fooling those around her. Still, her heart continued to break, but she had learned how to cry silently.

It was nearing the end of the two weeks Logan had suggested they wait. "Eleanor. We should talk to Ellery and David on Saturday."

Eleanor agreed. But the anxiety lay heavy on her heart, risking a confrontation where Logan was concerned. He's the love of her life and keeping him healthy and safe was her only priority. She would call Ellery tomorrow and invite them for pizza. Madison had a sleepover party to attend, so it would be the perfect time for a private meeting.

Logan opened the newspaper and Eleanor picked up the latest book she was reading. Both sat content in the tranquility of togetherness. A few hours later Eleanor opened her eyes and noticed that both she and Logan had fallen into a deep sleep.

He was still sleeping as she went to fix dinner. She smiled thinking of her husband. He was a simple man; strong in his faith, providing unconditional love and support to her. It was her time to be the support. She would carefully plan how she would tell Ellery and David.

Eleanor put two roast beef sandwiches on plates with potato chips and some ice tea. She carried in his plate, calling out to him that it was time to eat. Approaching his chair, she had a strange feeling inside that couldn't be explained. It wasn't butterflies, but a sickening, churning feeling. She shook off the feeling and touched his shoulder

"Logan, honey, time to eat." *He must really be in a deep sleep.* She set his plate on the side table and called his name again. "Logan." Still no response. Not even a stirring.

The hairs on her arms bristled and there was a knot in her stomach. She stood in front of him as panic immediately overcame her. There was no rising and falling of his chest. Nothing. Hands shaking, she laid her hand on his heart. Nothing. The nightmare was beginning. She searched for a pulse. Nothing. Frantically, she pulled him to the floor.

"Where's a phone? Where is a phone!" She didn't know why she was shouting, there was no one there to hear her cries for help. Eying the phone on his chair she grabbed it and dialed 911. Instinctively she began CPR, not knowing if it was too late or if she was doing it correctly. It didn't matter. She had to save him.

Chapter 2
Cold and Callous

As the paramedics worked on Logan and prepared him for transport, Eleanor called David. Her actions were robotic; gathering medications, phone numbers, her purse. The noise in the background seemed muffled. It was almost dreamlike. Watching them work on Logan she prayed they would breathe life back into him. *I'm not ready to lose him. He's my rock. He's my life. He can't die. Not yet.* She prayed for strength. She prayed for peace. She began to plead with God not to take him.

Arriving at the hospital, Ellery and David rushed to Eleanor. Trying to keep her emotions under control, Eleanor told them that he didn't make it. David, with the instinct and agility of a cat, grabbed Ellery as she collapsed. Madison cried out "no" and ran to one of the chairs burying her head in her hands. Helpless, Eleanor stood there watching her daughter deal with the sudden death of her father. David, too, was in shock. He lost his own father at such a young age, and Logan became a father to him, not merely a father-in-law. David led Ellery to the sofa, as Eleanor numbly followed.

A man stepped into the room, but stayed back, giving the family several minutes before introducing himself, as the hospital chaplain, Father Murphy. He was soft-spoken and full of compassion. Reaching out and taking Eleanor's hands, he prayed for comfort, and offered his assistance.

The three sat there, holding each other's hands. They were silent, each in their own thoughts. Madison stayed on the chair she had collapsed in earlier. Ellery finally broke the silence.

"Mom, what happened? Dad was so healthy, so strong. I can't believe he's gone."

Eleanor turned her body towards her daughter, eyes swollen and face colorless, knew the dreaded moment had arrived. She must now explain, without Logan here, what they had kept from everyone. It was time to tell her the truth. "Dad died of a massive heart attack. There was nothing anyone could do, even though they tried."

"A heart attack? He's not that old. How? Why?" Ellery was in disbelief.

Eleanor took a deep breath as she wrestled with finding just the right words. "Dad didn't want any of you to know how bad his heart was. The doctor told us last year that his heart wasn't strong. Bypass surgery would not help. We were told it could happen at any time or not for several years."

Ellery pulled away, jerking her hand from Eleanor's. "I don't believe you. You knew and didn't tell us! How could you be so selfish! How could you take what little time I had with Dad away from me?"

Eleanor's mouth grew dry, her eyes pleading. "It was your dad's wish. He didn't want sympathy or sad eyes at every family outing. He wanted to live a normal life and be treated as such. It was the hardest thing he ever asked me to do."

Ellery's once ashen face turned to a deep shade of red, neck veins pulsating and body rigid. "You should have told me! You should have told his daughter!"

Eleanor reached for her daughter. "Ellery…" Ellery pulled away and ran out of the room. As David rushed to follow her, he turned towards Eleanor. "Mom, how could you hurt her this way?"

"Would you please take care of them, Father Murphy?" Eleanor sat shaken and distraught.

Madison's heart was breaking, but her head was still very much in control. She enjoyed watching all of this unfold, and was pleased to be alone with her gramma. She heard it all - Gramma caused Grampa to die and also kept it a secret from Mom. Eyes swollen, but fixed and cold, she stood in front of her gramma, "You killed him. I wish you had died." She walked out of the room to find her parents. The stage was set for what would be her final act.

Eleanor sat alone in a room that was meant to offer consolation and support from those she loved, but found herself more alone than she could imagine. Logan was gone and Ellery may never forgive her. She knew her daughter would be upset, but nothing prepared her for the anger and contempt she witnessed. David also blamed her and Madison accused her of killing her grampa. More than Logan died today. A portion of the family died, too.

The thoughts about how to help a daughter who was angry and hurt, and a granddaughter who not only hated her but now blamed her for Logan's death, flooded her mind. *I knew losing Logan would be hard, but this... this I never expected... his secret may have destroyed our family. Do I even have enough tears to shed? Can I survive going through the motions of a funeral? Will Ellery ever believe, or even, forgive me?*

Eleanor prayed that by tomorrow her daughter's anger would subside enough that she and David would be ready to listen. Eleanor bowed her head and prayed for strength.

Strength to go on without her Logan. Strength to face her daughter. Strength to make the decisions needed. Strength to restore her relationship with Madison.

Eleanor turned, eyes and heart hopeful, as she heard the door open. But her heart sank even though she was glad to see Pastor Harris and Lisa. The pastor put his arms around her and immediately prayed for Eleanor to be comforted and the family to heal. "I spoke to Ellery outside. I'm sorry she is taking this so hard. She told me that you kept Logan's illness from her."

Eleanor nodded. "It was Logan's wish. No one knew except for his doctor and myself."

"It was a shock to lose her father unexpectedly and then finding out that his illness was kept from her. I'm sure she will calm down within the next few days." Pastor Harris said.

"Is there someone you would like to call to spend the night with you? Lisa asked.

Eleanor shook her head and said, "No. I will be fine. I have been preparing for this time to come." What she didn't plan on was being alone the first night. It was always an assumption that Ellery or Madison would be with her. She didn't want to tell them about Madison. Logan was the only person she had confided in and now he was gone.

Father Murphy returned. "I'm so sorry for your loss and for the family turmoil." He paused to introduce himself to

Pastor Harris, before continuing. "Your daughter and family left. But, they were able to say their goodbyes before leaving. I will be here tomorrow if you should need me for anything."

She thanked Father Murphy for his kindness and said she would call on him if needed. Eleanor went to see Logan one last time before having the Harris' drive her home. The ride home seemed to take forever and she was glad they understood she needed to be left in her thoughts. Pulling into the driveway, Pastor Harris broke the silence. "Eleanor, please call us if you need anything. Lisa and I are available anytime, day or night. We can be here in fifteen minutes."

Eleanor thanked them. Pastor Harris again prayed Eleanor would be comforted and able to get rest. She got out of the car, unlocked her door, and waved to signal she was inside. Only then, did they drive away.

The house was dark with only street lights shining through the windows. Somehow this was fitting given the events of the day. She felt for the kitchen light switch. Eleanor looked around and saw her sandwich still sitting on the counter. Loud sobs shook her body, as she stumbled to the dinette chair.

"Oh Logan," Eleanor cried out. "Why now? Why did we keep this secret? I am so alone. We always thought that Ellery, David, and Madison would be here to comfort me and help me get through the first night. Logan, you have abandoned me. Not on purpose, but you are gone, and our daughter has turned her back on me at a time when I need her the most."

Sobs continued to engulf her body, as though she was being sucked down to the bottom of the ocean. She couldn't break free, she couldn't breathe, she couldn't move. She could only see life moving past her. It was some time before she was released from the ocean floor.

She walked to the bedroom and looked at the bed they had shared for nearly forty-five years. She turned and walked to the family room. Logan's chair was the first thing she saw. The television was still on and the side table overturned. She couldn't bear to be in this room, either. She turned off the television, walked to the living room and sat on the sofa. She was tired, cold, and numb. Taking the afghan from the back of the sofa, she laid down, and closed her eyes.

Sleep was intermittent throughout the night. Faces seemed to enter each dream. Logan, Ellery, David, Madison, the emergency crew, and the doctors. The house was dark except for the light she left on in the kitchen. Just when she thought sleep was near, the sun started peeking through the drapes.

Eleanor went to the closet for a fresh outfit. She washed her face and ran a brush through her hair. She picked up her purse and opened the door, but stopped. *Should I call Ellery or let her contact me when she's ready?* She backed away from the door and dialed the number.

David picked up on the third ring. "Hello."

"Hello, David. Is Ellery around?" Either Ellery didn't want to answer or she was away from her phone.

"She's in the shower. What do you need?" His voice was cold and distant.

Eleanor began to speak, "Um...I...I...wanted to see ...um...to see...how she was doing and if she wanted to meet me at the funeral home to make the arrangements."

"I'll ask her, but I doubt it. I'll have her call you. Bye." David hung up the phone.

The phone clicked before Eleanor could even get a thank you or goodbye out. She sat at the table and waited. The phone finally rang. Anxiously, she answered on the first ring. "Hello."

"Eleanor. David here. She's not ready to speak to you yet. You should just make whatever arrangements you want. Bye." Again, David hung up before Eleanor had a chance to say anything.

The battle of the tears continued. *Is it my imagination or did he sound insensitive? He never offered any words of comfort or sympathy. This has been a shock to everyone, so maybe I'm reading too much into what he said and how he said it.* She took a deep breath and said a quick prayer that God would help her get through all the arrangements that had to be made; alone.

Eleanor took time to straighten the area around Logan's chair. She picked up the overturned side table and food that had fallen on the floor. Walking out the door, she realized a good jolt of caffeine was needed. Food would have to wait. Not that she wasn't hungry, but because her stomach was a roller coaster of emotions. She hoped that maybe after all the decisions were made, she could eat.

Eleanor slowly shuffled one leaded foot in front of the other, as she made her way to the funeral home door. She and Logan had already made the formal arrangements months ago, but today the journey would begin sealing closed their life together.

Logan had wished to be cremated, with no service, unless she or Ellery needed or wanted one. His only request, that it be a small service. He would say, "I want your last memories of me to be full of life and not a funeral."

The funeral home had agreed to wait until tomorrow to cremate the body. This would give Ellery the opportunity to see her dad one last time, if she chose to. Eleanor would return next week to pick up the urn with his ashes. *I'm still not sure what to do with the urn or where to put it. He served in Vietnam and should be honored for that. Maybe I'll check into a military cemetery for his interment. I'll get Ellery's opinion, that is, if she forgives me.*

It was time to pack up Logan's belongings. As she held the navy suit, she thought of Logan looking so distinguished as he set out to work every day. She could see him on the treadmill as she folded a pair of sweat pants. It had been a month since Logan's death and still the smell of his after shave lingered on his shirts. The lasagna stain on his favorite sweater reminded her of the time they went to eat at the new Italian restaurant in town. Everything had a memory. She made a pile to donate and a pile to keep for a later decision. She also had a pile for Ellery and David, hoping they would soon forgive her enough to communicate.

She hadn't heard from them since the night Logan died. *I can't wait any longer. If they won't forgive me or even talk to me, I'll just set the date. I need to know if they want to attend his burial at the military cemetery.* Eleanor had found the cemetery only thirty miles away. They would do a simple service with honor guard. She was holding off on the date waiting for Ellery.

Before she lost her nerve, she dialed. One ring. Two rings. Three rings. Four rings. Voice mail. "Hello. This is Mom. Hope you are all well. I would like to schedule Dad's burial. Let me know dates that would work for you. I love you all." Eleanor hung up the phone with a sense of despair.

David and Ellery listened to the message. Ellery looked at David. "What do you think? Should we give my mom some dates and attend?"

"It's up to you, but I can't attend. She hurt all of us, but mostly you. How do we know your dad wanted everything kept from us? Madison seems to be happy without your mom around. That should tell us something." David replied.

"Agreed. But, I would like to have closure and this could be it. What do you think? We don't have to talk with her." Ellery seemed almost pleading. "I think Madison needs to have closure, too."

"Okay. But text her with dates. Make it clear that this is for you and Madison to have closure and nothing more."

"Thank you, David. I'll send the text later, after I look at the calendar."

Eleanor was nervous as she waited for them to arrive. Six chairs were set out. Four in front for the immediate family and then two behind, for Pastor Harris and Lisa. The empty stand was centered and draped in a simple white cloth. The Army liaison had gone through the order in which things would be done. The final, and perhaps hardest for her, would be the presentation of the flag.

David, Ellery, and Madison arrived five minutes before the ceremony. They nodded to Eleanor as they took their seats. Eleanor smiled as she stood with outstretched arms.

But, that was not to be. A coldness fell on what had started to be a warm day as David, with immediate defiance, took the chair next to Eleanor. The three Weber's sat with no visible greeting or comfort for Eleanor. No one said a word. No one returned the smile or even looked at Eleanor.

Lisa's stomach was churning. She wanted to wrap her arms around her dear friend and save her from the impending attack. Pastor bowed his head and prayed for peace. Eleanor didn't hide the tears. She let them flow freely. They flowed for Logan. They flowed for her loss of family.

The ceremony began in typical military fashion. Precision. No mistakes. It was solemn and the Army Chaplin spoke words of a grateful nation and how Logan had served his country. The honor guard folded the flag and presented it to Eleanor. She hung her head and let Logan's flag become saturated with grief.

Her peripheral vision alerted her that those she needed to lean on continued to be detached from all emotion. She sat alone, void of any comfort.

The ceremony was over. Ellery spoke for the first time. "It was a nice service, Mother. Thank you for including us." She stepped back to allow Madison to speak to her gramma.

"I hate you. You killed Grampa. You've been mean to me and I won't ever forgive you for hitting me, either. I wish you were dead."

Pastor Harris moved towards Eleanor, but she put her hand up to stop him. She fought against her legs buckling. "I never hit you," her voice soft and quivering as she continued, "I was never mean to you, and we both know I didn't kill…" but before Eleanor could finish, Madison had already walked away.

David paused before stepping closer to Eleanor. His words were callused and well-rehearsed. "Madison told us how you have been treating her. How you hit her when we were out of town. How you didn't want her to visit Grampa. Dad may have physically died, but you Eleanor," David leaned closer in an intimidating manner before finishing, "are also dead to us." He turned and the three, arm in arm, walked away. Madison turned her head and stared before flashing a proud smile.

An eerie silence settled over the cemetery. No one said a word.

Eleanor stood in frozen silence. Her bloodless face bore eyes that were fixed and glazed. She started rubbing her arms, trying to unthaw the blizzard of hate and contempt that had just been thrown at her.

This is a nightmare! Surely Ellery and David won't believe Madison. They must know how well she can lie.

Eleanor's mouth opened but she couldn't form any words. She was speechless. She should defend herself. She

27

should explain. But, she just shook her head. Pastor Harris rushed to Eleanor's side as she slumped down into the chair. Lisa knelt before her. "What can we do? Lisa asked.

"I don't think anyone can do anything. They blame me for not telling them about Logan's heart condition. They believe it was my idea to keep it from them and I made Logan go along with it." Even though she was outside, Eleanor couldn't find enough air to breathe.

Lisa was talking, she knew because she could see her mouth moving, but the words were all jumbled. "Eleanor." Lisa gently shook her arm. "Do you want me to drive you home?"

"No...I mean...yes. Did I drive? Yes. Yes, I did. I'm sorry. I seem to be in a fog. I need to apologize for the family's behavior today. If I had known there would be so much animosity today, I wouldn't have invited them. Logan didn't deserve this.

Pastor Harris took control. "Lisa will drive you home." Eleanor nodded slightly. It was as if she had forgotten how to walk and needed to rely on their steady support. It was to be a long drive home.

Chapter 3
Unwanted Escape

It was an endless day. She roamed the house sitting first in his favorite chair, caressing the arms. Oh, how he loved his chair where he spent hours watching sports or reading. She twisted the wedding ring he had placed on her finger so many years ago and the vows they made. Eleanor moved to the bedroom and sat on his side of the bed. She ran her fingers over the family picture. She picked up his Bible and held it to her chest. His faith held them together throughout the years, especially during the bad times.

Every item she saw and touched reminded her of Logan. Every room held a memory. But every room also held memories of Ellery. Their only child. She was so special to them, and now she was gone.

How could this happen? I don't know if I can go on living here. I've lost my world. I'm alone. Totally alone.

Two months and no communication from Ellery. Time to confront and face what may be her future without Ellery. Eleanor didn't bother to call. She got in her car and drove twenty minutes to Ellery's house. Her legs begged to run as she knocked on the door, but before she could put them into motion, the door opened.

"What do you want, Mother?" The reception was frosty, at best and Ellery's eyes bore no warmth.

Mother? She only called me mother when she was angry. Eleanor swallowed hard. "May I please come in?"

"There's nothing to say. But, if you insist." Ellery stepped aside in a brisk and business-like manner to allow Eleanor to enter.

David walked in. "What is Eleanor doing here?" His eyes narrowed, jaw set, shoulders pulled back, and fists clenched ready to strike. It was still the harsh, hard-hearted tone he had used before.

"She wants to talk. I told her we didn't have anything to say." Ellery muttered furiously.

"Okay. Speak, Eleanor." David barked.

"Maybe we should sit down while we talk." Eleanor timidly suggested.

David's words were emotionless and exact. "No need.

You won't be staying long. Just say what you've come to say and then leave our house."

Eleanor looked at Ellery and saw a statue, rigid and unmoving. "Alright. I want to apologize again for the hurt. Dad didn't want anyone to know and I respected that. We both thought he would have time."

Ellery refused to let her mother continue. "Mother. I find it hard to believe that Dad wouldn't share something like this with me."

David flew into a boisterous rage. "You can't expect us to believe you. You abused our daughter when we weren't around. And not just words, you were physical. You denied her time with Logan. Yet, you stand there and want us to believe you? You make me sick! Get out of our house forever!"

Eleanor once again lacked the words for defense. She looked at Ellery. The unresponsive statute hadn't changed. Ellery opened the door. "I think you best leave Mother. David speaks for all of us. Don't come back. Don't call. Don't write."

There was nothing left. She walked out; not looking back. She was being expelled from her family. The only family she had left in this world. Eleanor wanted to vomit. Again, the same thoughts went through her mind. *How could all of this be happening to me? First Logan dies, Ellery doesn't believe me, and now Madison's cruel lies. Why wasn't I more forceful in defending myself?*

She pounded her fists on the steering wheel. *Oh, Logan. Why are you making me face this alone?* The drive home was stuck in slow motion; the traffic, her car, and her mind. Her thoughts, though, came in rapid fire. *What should I do? Should I continue to deny Madison's claims and try to talk to Ellery and David again? No. They said to stay out of their lives. Their anger was louder than the words. For now, I will do nothing.*

Once inside the house, she made her way into the family room and collapsed in her chair. Her body was ravaged by so many emotions. She thought losing Logan was going to be the hardest thing she would have to deal with, but now this too, in less than four months. Her heart had been broken multiple times through this ordeal, and she wasn't sure this time it would heal. It felt like someone cut her heart into thousands of unsalvageable pieces and threw them into a bottomless cavern. She somehow stumbled into the bedroom, laid down, and wept until she fell asleep.

Morning arrived after a restless night. She slowly made her way to the kitchen for a much needed cup of coffee. She sat at the counter praying the phone would ring. She wanted to have her family back. She wanted her granddaughter back in her life, back to the times where they laughed and played games together. She thought about confiding in someone, but decided to deal with it alone.

It was time to meet with her attorney and change the joint trust fund to a single trust fund. The office had left a message last week regarding papers that needed to be signed. Jake came in with the file and offered the usual condolences. He had been their legal representative and friend for nearly twenty years.

"Eleanor. I know you think this is simply signing some forms and putting the trust into your name, but Logan had a separate account, naming you as the beneficiary. He also left me a letter to give to you." Jake said.

"A separate account? Logan never mentioned any such thing." Eleanor was confused.

Jake explained. "Logan opened the account when he started getting substantial raises. He had the money deducted from his paycheck. With each raise he would have more money withheld and invested."

Eleanor was dumbfounded. "Jake. I had no idea. I don't know what to say."

"No need to say anything right now. Today we need to complete the paperwork for your trust, and sign the separate account over to you. It's a good sum. The letter is personal. You may want to read it in private."

She looked at the paperwork in front of her. There were

two accounts, one was for her and the other for Ellery. Eleanor was in disbelief as she looked at the account Logan left her. "Oh my! Oh my! This can't be. There must be a mistake!"

"I thought you might respond that way. Money seems to grow when invested. You look like you want to ask if this is for real. Yes. It is. As you see, your account is worth a total of two-hundred fifty thousand dollars." Jake said.

"I'm a bit confused. This is separate from his pension? What about his social security?" Eleanor now had a flood of questions. This meeting was no longer just a formality.

Jake cleared his throat. "Well. Let me take your questions one at a time. You will get seventy-five percent of his pension. As far as social security, you need to make an appointment and find out what your options are. You also have your pension."

"So, financially. What am I looking at?" Eleanor asked.

"Somewhere in the ballpark of a little over a half-million dollars in savings. This doesn't include your monthly income." Jake said.

The meeting over, Eleanor went home. She couldn't believe Logan did this for her. Her selfless, wonderful husband. He didn't know then that he would die so early in life, but he planned to take care of her no matter what. She took out the letter and read it slowly several times. Logan talked about his love for her, the memories, and the beautiful life he had because of her. He talked about Ellery and the bond the family had. A large lump formed in her throat. *If he only knew.*

Amazing. I slept through the night. It must have been from pure emotional exhaustion and nothing else. Hearing her stomach making the "I need food" sounds, she contemplated what to fix for breakfast. Realizing she hadn't eaten much lately, she poured a cup of coffee and sipped on it while making scrambled eggs and toast. Nourishing, she thought, but light on the stomach. She only wished she could find something that would be light on the heart.

Spending time cleaning the house gave Eleanor opportunity to clear her mind, to some extent. Too much time had been spent crying and feeling sorry for herself. Two weeks had passed since the exchange with Ellery and David, and still no communication them. It was time for a plan, a plan for her to move on with life. Logan would want that and he would be the first to say so. *Am I being too hasty? Should I even consider making drastic changes in my life?* Eleanor started making a list of possible changes.

Time to move forward. Too many reminders for the heart. I have been thrown out of the family. If I stay here, I may not heal, it may keep me from moving forward. If they don't want me, then I will get out of their lives forever.

I need to make a list of what items I really want and need. Most of the furniture and tools can stay or be sold. Where do I want to live? Tropical sounds nice, but I do like the seasons. I'll look at an atlas tonight and decide north or south, tropic or stateside. Her mind continued to wander from one thing to the next.

I need to find someone who isn't from around here, and who can be very discrete to sell the house and most of its belongings. How do I move the things I want to take with me? So many decisions to make, but, am I ready? Yes. I think I am. But, is this what is best or am I running away? Either way, it's what I have to do.

Eleanor made a preliminary list of what she wanted to take and another of what to sell. Now, the decision of where to live. Eleanor looked at the map, including places outside of the United States, while she ate her sandwich.

In just a few weeks Eleanor had listed her house. She hired a company to sell any remaining items.

It was the second letter from the same law office within two weeks. At first, Ellery thought it was junk mail. But now she was curious. It was from her dad's attorney regarding his will. She called David in from the garage to show him the letter. "What do you think? Should we call?"

David finished reading the letter carefully. "No. I think it's Eleanor's way of getting us in the same room again. The attorney probably knows nothing about it."

"You really think she would do that?" Ellery wasn't sure her mom was that conniving.

"Yes. I do. Besides we leave in a few days for vacation. If this is legit, they'll call. We'll know for sure when we get back. Deal?"

"Deal."

Pastor Harris and his wife came by to see Eleanor. They talked about Logan and how she was doing. Eleanor decided to let them know she was leaving. "I'm telling you both in confidence. I don't want anyone to know of my decision to move. Not church members, not neighbors, and most definitely not Ellery."

"But why, Eleanor? You have this beautiful house and church members who love you. Ellery will come around." Lisa said.

"Too many memories. I need to start new. I went to see David and Ellery. They told me to get out of their lives forever. I wasn't allowed to even sit down. I had to speak my peace in the foyer. No. It's time to move on." Eleanor said with sadness and defeat in her voice. "I haven't made any definite decisions yet, as to where I'm moving to, only that I'm selling the house."

Pastor Harris joined the conversation. "Are you absolutely sure you don't want me to talk to Ellery? Lisa and I can go together."

"No. Please don't." Eleanor begged. "When Ellery is ready, she will find me. Until then, I am going to move on with my life. My new life."

Eleanor chose not to disclose that her move wasn't just to a new house, but she may leave the country. Why make them worry. They talked for a while longer before leaving. After hugs and prayers, they wished her well and asked her to keep in touch.

The basement was the last to go through. Her art supplies and kiln were stored here. She had taught art years ago and until recently, spent many hours painting and drawing. She missed it. *No matter what the expense, my art supplies and* kiln *are going with me.*

Everything was packed and the truck would arrive in the morning. Her belongings should be to her new home within a week. She found a three-bedroom, two-bath condo overlooking the Caribbean Sea and within walking distance to shops and restaurants. Her requirements were simple; warm weather, beautiful beaches, and no poisonous snakes or scorpions. She purchased the condo after seeing online photos. It looked perfect. It was more than she planned on spending, but it was the perfect size, location, and it was available.

An offer on her home came a week after it was listed for several thousand over market value. The buyer wanted to purchase the furniture and be able to take possession within thirty days. This was an answer to prayer and made the moving easier. Things had moved quickly. Eleanor would soon be on a plane headed to St. Croix, in the U.S. Virgin Islands, by early next week. No time for second thoughts.

They boarded the plane, excited to finally have some down time. Madison couldn't believe she was going to New York City and getting a break from school. The hotel was near Time Square making it easy to enjoy shows, shopping, and sight-seeing that were all on the agenda. Ellery was looking forward to having a distraction from her dad's death and her mother's deceitfulness. David was happy to sleep in and not worry about work. Each of them had their different reasons for wanting this vacation.

A few hours later they were making their way to the hotel. David had pulled out all the stops. They had two adjoining rooms overlooking the city. They were so excited to get out and see the sights, so they set the suitcases down, grabbed cameras, sunglasses, light jackets, and ran out to see New York City.

After the New York trip, David and Ellery were going to Cancun. Just the two of them. It was an early anniversary trip. Madison would stay with their close family friends, the Richardson's. Their daughter, Angela, was Madison's best friend.

Only a few hours remained before Eleanor boarded her plane for a new beginning. David made it very clear not to contact them, but she needed to make one last attempt. Looking out the window and then at the clock, Eleanor fidgeted with the buttons on her jacket. Time was going by slowly as she sat waiting for the shuttle to take her to the airport. She was afraid to try one last time to call her only child, but time was running out.

Picking up her phone, she punched in Ellery's number, knowing it was now or never. She exhaled loudly as it started to ring. Three rings, four rings, and no answer. Finally, she heard the voice mail greeting, "Hello, this is Ellery. I'm unable to take your call at this time, please leave a message."

Eleanor spoke only three words - "I love you." Picking up her purse, she left the room.

Chapter 4
The Message

Sitting at the table, the Weber's were enjoying a relaxing breakfast in the hotel restaurant. Today they were going to the Statue of Liberty and the Empire State Building. Ellery's phone started to buzz and all three of them noticed the caller. She looked at David wondering if she should answer it. David's face tightened as he shook his head no. Ellery was relieved she didn't have to make the decision. The ringing finally stopped, and in a few seconds the sound went off to notify them that the caller had left a message.

"Do you think we should listen to the message in case it's an emergency? I don't think she would call for any other reason." Ellery said.

"Go ahead. Put it on speaker for all of us to hear."

She played the brief message, "I love you."

David spoke in a low tone; his voice becoming venomous. "Of all the nerve! I specifically told her not to communicate. She's trying to manipulate you into running back to her and forgiving her for what she did!"

Ellery choked back her emotions, "I don't know what to think anymore. Maybe she's just lonely. Maybe she wants to try for our forgiveness again. Maybe she just wants us to know that, no matter what, forgiveness or not, she loves us."

"There is no forgiveness and there won't be. She can do her guilty calls, but we won't be forgiving any time soon. If it's an emergency, someone will inform us. Her pastor knows the situation." David looked at Ellery with a hardness in his eyes she hadn't noticed before.

The conversation was over and gone was any hope of reuniting with her mother. Ellery was beginning to soften towards her mother. She thought they had punished her enough. Madison saw the loneliness in her mother's eyes and wondered if maybe she had taken this too far. She quickly pushed the thoughts aside, her head taking over her heart.

It had been a wonderful vacation. A vacation that allowed her to forget the turmoil in her life, but now she was back and she became more and more miserable. She missed her mom more than anything, but David and Madison convinced her that Eleanor was still a danger to them. She longed to confide in someone. She wanted someone to tell her what to do; that her mom was not a villain. David was firm, insisting none of them would have any communication with Eleanor.

Ellery watched David with Madison. It seemed the two of them were living a different life, and she was observing through the window. It was a giant game of tug-of-war. She was in the middle with David and Madison pulling on one side, and her heart pulling just as hard from the other side. She had lost one parent from a heart attack, and now the other parent because of deceit and accusations. She ached to drive by the house to just see her mom, but with David being so adamant about no contact, she knew that was impossible. Her mind continued to drift.

I wish I knew mom's neighbors. Most of them are new and have only lived in the area for a short time. My parents were the last of the close-knit group of neighbors from the cul-de-sac. It's too risky to drive by the house. What if my mom saw me? I don't want her to think all is forgiven and life will get back to normal. David has no intention of forgiving, and Madison seems happier without my mom in the picture. I am torn into so many pieces.

I remember so many times Mom being there for me, giving words of wisdom. My best friend believed lies about me and vowed never to speak to me again. I ran home in tears, devastated. Mom listened to me and held me close, before telling me that no matter how many lies are told, or for how long, at some point, they will be found out. Mistakes will be made and their words will be shown for all to see. She told me not to fear because God won't let them destroy me.

Mom reminded me that Jesus demands us to love our enemies. She said to show kindness, love them and forgive them.

I said, "I'd try."

Mom simply replied, "It will take some time, but it won't last forever. This may be a good time to make new friends, but not to give up your old friends. Be ready to forgive, and most importantly, forget."

Ellery continued to think about all the other times her mom had been there for her. The advice was always the same, be kind, have faith, and trust God. It was good advice, and advice she should be using now. She needs to show kindness and love unconditionally to David, Madison and her mom. Her regret in all of this, is that she can't offer it to her mom, the person she so wants most to show kindness to. Maybe in a few more months David will change his mind and she can at least talk to her mom on the phone.

"Ellery, Ellery." David kept saying.

"Mom?" Madison said.

Hearing her name being called brought her thoughts to a screeching halt. Ellery looked up surprised to see both David and Madison staring at her with puzzled faces. "I'm sorry. I must have been daydreaming."

"What were you daydreaming about? You were really into it." David wanted to know.

"Well, it was about Sheila, an old friend in middle school, and a disagreement we once had. It all worked out in the end. It's her birthday in a few days and I got lost in old memories. Remind me to pick up a birthday card and get it in the mail." She paused and saw they were both looking at her with huge grins on their faces. "The two of you seem to want my attention. Any specific reason?"

David and Madison laughed before David responded. "We wanted to know if you had any plans today. Madison and I thought it would be nice to go to the mall and get some Christmas shopping done."

"That sounds like fun. I can be ready in thirty minutes; how long will it take you guys?" Ellery asked.

"Well, I'm almost ready, so only a few. Hey, isn't Sheila the friend you always call or send a card to this time of year? How could have forgotten her birthday?" David asked.

"I don't know. Maybe I was too busy thinking about Christmas, decorations, parties, and gifts." Ellery sent a playful wink to David.

The mall was crowded, as always, several weeks before Christmas. The three decided to each go their own way and then meet up in two hours for lunch. David and Madison immediately headed to the second floor. Ellery was glad to have time to herself so she could think and shop without the two of them telling her to look at this, every two minutes.

Ellery took the list out of her purse and reviewed it. She decided to first get the birthday card for Sheila and then definitely call her later. Next on the list was David. She needed to look for a blue sweater and a set of golf clubs. He had been throwing enough hints to fill up a dart board.

She also had to shop for David's sister, brother-in-law and two nephews. Last on the list were the Secret Santa gifts for work and church. She was glad that David would help her shop for Madison. As she set out to complete her list, sadness crept in as she remembered there wouldn't be shopping for either of her parents this year.

David and Madison were equally as busy shopping for Ellery. They found a nice watch and necklace, but they were still searching for a combination sewing and embroidery machine. David said they may need to go outside the mall to find it. He knew Ellery was taking care of his family so that left work and Madison's friends and the school party.

The food court was already crowded as Ellery searched for David and Madison. David's height made it easier to spot him waving. She worked through the maze of shoppers to where they were standing.

"Wow, I think everyone decided to eat at the same time." David said. "Are we done at the mall or does anyone have more shopping to do?"

"I'm done, Dad," said Madison.

"I'm done and done in," laughed Ellery.

"Great. Instead of fighting the hungry crowds, let's leave the mall and head for a restaurant on the way home. My stomach is telling me it's tired of waiting for nourishment. Sound good?" David asked.

"Sounds good," both ladies said in unison.

Ellery smiled. It was a good day. Relaxed, after a tumultuous few months, excitement and anticipation filled her soul. Happy thoughts of baking, wrapping, parties to attend and host no longer felt a burden. She was even looking forward to all of Madison's events.

They chose one of their favorite restaurants only a few blocks from home, which offered something for each of them. Ellery knew her family well and predicted that Madison would get either a pizza or a hamburger with fries, David would order a steak, and she would get the wet burrito. Once seated, they all sighed and then laughed.

"I guess we were all ready to call it a day," Ellery said. "Now, let's order. I'm starved!"

Later that evening, Ellery called her friend to wish her a happy birthday and then joined Madison and David to watch a movie and eat popcorn. A perfect ending to a much needed perfect day.

Her plane landed late in the day, after a few delays. It was overcast as she stepped outside, a little apprehensive to be in a different country and to start a new life in a home she had yet to see. She looked around hoping that her realtor would be there to help ease the tension building inside her. She was tired, both from travel and nerves.

"Mrs. Morgan?" Said a tall, young woman with long brown hair. Not thinking Eleanor heard her, she repeated, "Mrs. Morgan?" Eleanor turned and waved, as the young lady said, "I'm Amaya Diaz."

"Yes, I'm Mrs. Morgan. It's so nice to finally meet you in person. I'm sorry it's so late, I had a few flight delays."

"That happens, Amaya said with a smile. "Let me help you with your luggage, Mrs. Morgan."

"Thank you. And please call me Eleanor."

"I will do that and please call me Amaya. I imagine you are tired from all the traveling. My car is over there. It's about a forty-five minute ride to your condo. Not far according to island travel."

Amaya put the luggage in the car and asked, "Are you hungry or thirsty?"

"Yes, to both. I would love to stop and get something to eat, but I'm also anxious to see my new home. Is there a place we can get take-out? Guess I'm somewhat impatient." Eleanor replied.

"I understand. There is a wonderful little store and deli close to your condo." Amaya said.

"That sounds ideal." Eleanor replied.

"I'm sure you are looking forward to relaxing after your long trip, so I will give you as much information as I can on the way to the condo. Your area is a mix of well-established families, new residents, and tourists." Amaya continued.

"You must do this a lot or you have ESP," Eleanor said.

Amaya laughed and said, "I wish it was ESP, but I have many clients who move here or purchase vacation property. I also love to travel and know after a day of traveling, I just want my chair, food, and a good movie."

It was Eleanor's turn to laugh. "It's nice to know my realtor is so in tune with her clients."

"Well, I try. I'm sure you have many questions, so I will try to answer most of them before you ask. I prepared a folder with maps of the island and your community. You will also find a list of restaurants, shops, businesses, churches, and emergency numbers. There is a second folder containing all the manuals and important information regarding your condo and the association."

Amaya continued to talk about the island, weather, beaches, and things to do. She was definitely answering all the questions. They stopped at the small store where Eleanor ordered a sandwich and then grabbed an armful of junk food and soft drinks.

As they pulled into the driveway of the condo, Eleanor released the breath she had been holding. "This is beautiful. Are you sure this is mine?"

Smiling, Amaya gave her a few minutes to take it all in. "The condos are close together, but each has a fenced front yard, for privacy and privacy fences on each side. The back overlooks the Caribbean Sea. Shall we get out and see the condo? I'll help you with your luggage later."

"By all means. Let's see my new home." Eleanor said, jumping out of the car with a new burst of energy.

They opened the front gate and entered a covered walkway. The front yard wasn't very big, but large enough for a small garden. The walkway was tiled and the frame was painted a bright yellow. The door opened to a large entrada, known as a foyer in the states, with travertine tiled floors, which continued throughout the condo. To the left was a brightly frescoed dining room and to the right an open-concept kitchen and family room. The kitchen and family room allowed sweeping views of the Caribbean Sea and beach, largely due to the two sets of French doors opening to the covered patio. She envisioned herself sitting here watching the sunset each evening. The family room led to a small den with doors leading to the same patio. The room had a warm and cozy feel.

Back in the hallway, Eleanor made her way to two large en suite master bedrooms, each with their own entrance to the outside. A third bedroom, much smaller than the other two, housed her neatly stacked boxes.

The vast amount of windows and covered patio spaces released a new world to her. A world of light, water and sand. Eleanor was mesmerized.

"This is more beautiful than the pictures. I thought it was going to be much smaller, but I'm delighted at the size. The tile floors and bright colors are so different from what I am accustomed too, but, I love it! And it's furnished." Eleanor was beaming.

Amaya nodded, waiting to see if Eleanor had more to say. After a minute of silence, she said, "Eleanor, welcome home. I'm sure you would love to eat your sandwich and put your feet up, so let's get your luggage and I'll be on my way."

"I do think my feet are ready for that chair and my body for some overdo nourishment." Eleanor laughed, giving Amaya a big hug.

"Have a restful night and welcome to the island. Please call anytime." Amaya walked to her car and Eleanor closed the door.

Eleanor sat back and relaxed for the first time in two days. Alone in a new house, a new city, and a new country. She gave a sigh. Once again, she was overwhelmed and alone; but thankful.

She awakened early to the sound of the waves. It took her a minute to remember she was in a new house. Smiling, she stood and saw a wrinkled mess in the mirror. She opened the blinds to let the morning sun fill the room. Having forgotten there was a patio off the bedroom she opened the doors and took in the warm breeze. The sea was fairly calm as she spanned the area. The bedroom patio connected to the same one as the den and family room.

Remembering there was a second large bedroom, she went to see if it too, had a patio. Opening the doors and stepping on to the patio Eleanor was excited. *I bet if I put a divider of some kind between the two bedroom patios, I could have a private oasis.* Looking closer, she saw the privacy fence Amaya had mentioned separating the condominiums. *This, is my bedroom and I'll use the other master bedroom for my studio. The smaller bedroom is for guests, should I ever get any, and additional storage. But first, I need to get out of this wrinkled mess.*

Now, where did I leave my luggage? Oh, yes, in the dining room. Quickly retrieving her luggage, she decided a shower was in order. She was grateful the realtor had suggested that she pack a towel in her suitcase.

Showered and a set of fresh clothes, Eleanor made her way to the kitchen in hopes there was instant coffee hidden in the cupboard. A thorough search of every cupboard had the same ending-no coffee. A coffee maker was located, but nothing to put in it. She had given no thought to food or coffee last night when she was at the store. *No food and no coffee. I can't believe I didn't think to buy coffee last night, just the immediate desire for junk food.* Opening the refrigerator, Eleanor took out a bottle of water and went to the patio, enjoying the ocean air.

Picking up the map Amaya left, Eleanor headed to town. She was going to first find a restaurant and get a good breakfast and a hot cup of coffee. She located a quaint restaurant that was already buzzing with customers. Finding a table near the front window she picked up a menu, determined to find something to eat. Eleanor wanted to try all the local cuisine, but today it needed to be something her stomach could manage.

Smiling, she thought of Logan and his urging to keep up with her Spanish. She was thankful for that advice. Spanish had been her minor in college, but the thought never crossed her mind that she would one day live someplace where she would need to speak it daily.

Eleanor enjoyed watching the people walk by as she ate. Breakfast finished, she returned to the sidewalk and looked at the quaint shops that lined the streets, all painted in vibrant colors. Most of them were begging for her to step inside to see their treasures. She longed to get lost in each of them. But, the grocery store came first. Not as enticing, but very much a necessity.

Amaya had mentioned that for a small fee, most stores deliver. Before Eleanor began her shopping, she inquired first if they provided delivery service and if they delivered to her address. Up and down each aisle, she crossed items off her list. She also chose several things she didn't need, giving into temptation. She stopped at the meat counter, selecting some fresh fish and meat, then the bakery for bread and donuts.

She longed to see the rest of the town and browse in the shops, but her order was being delivered within the next hour. *Maybe tomorrow. Today I need to get home before the delivery is made and begin the task of unpacking. The day is warming up fast. Thank goodness for the breeze or this walk would already be uncomfortable.* Walking allowed her to become more acquainted with her new community. She was anxious to see even more, but getting settled was priority.

Eleanor began to unpack the luggage that she brought on the plane. There was plenty of room for clothes in the dresser and in the large walk-in closet. She had been working on putting things away when the doorbell rang. *Groceries,* she thought, as she rushed to the door.

"You must be new to the island," the young delivery man said. "Do you know you can call in your order for delivery without coming into the store?"

"I didn't know that. Thank you. I might do that on a rainy day." Eleanor thanked him for delivering her groceries so quickly and for the information.

She took time to put the groceries away before returning to the task of unpacking. She loved having the doors opened to the patio and allowing the fresh air and gentle breezes to flow through the condo. Once the suitcases were empty, she went to see what boxes to unpack first. Standing there, it was obvious she needed more room to move around and organize, so she cleared out all of the boxes marked art supplies and carried them to what would be her studio, putting them in the closet until she figured out what to do with the furniture.

Moving the art boxes definitely made the room less crowded and easier to sort through them. She was glad she chose to pack in smaller boxes, as it made lifting and carrying a much easier task. She's not sure how she would have managed larger and heavier boxes by herself. Finally, locating the kitchen boxes, she carried them to the dining room table. The large table made it the perfect sorting area to organize her kitchen.

After about an hour of sorting and organizing, Eleanor stopped for a light lunch. Taking her salad, fresh baked roll, and water to the patio, she sat facing the water where she could watch people walking along the beach.

Her condo sat between two public beaches, allowing anyone to walk from one beach to the other. Eleanor watched several people, she assumed were neighbors, getting ready to relax and enjoy themselves, as they put up umbrellas and set out their towels. She hoped to meet them soon.

I do love sitting here, but the boxes won't unpack themselves. While unpacking the last few kitchen boxes, she thought about some items she may need. Kitchen done, she returned to the small bedroom to figure out what to unpack next. The room that was once overflowing with boxes looked a lot thinner. Still, there was much to tackle.

Chapter 5
New Surroundings

She was glad that Amaya had found someone to purchase the bedroom furniture before the boxes had been shipped. Being able to store all the boxes in one room was better than having them strewn throughout the condo. She planned to move the furniture from her future studio in once she emptied it from all the boxes.

Eleanor worked on boxes for the next several hours before calling it a day. She was tired of carrying, opening, and organizing. She needed fresh air and the beach was calling to her.

The sand felt wonderful to her feet as she made her way to the water, which was warm and clear. She strolled along the shore for the next twenty minutes or so before turning back. The walk gave her renewed energy as she drank in the views and serenity. She loved the sunshine, the breeze, and the waves striking against her legs.

Close enough to see her condo, she was in awe that it belonged to her. A little of that happiness seemed to wash back out to sea, as cloud of sadness came over her, knowing that Logan was not here to share it. She knew he was in a better place, no longer tired or weak, but still she longed to have him here walking beside her.

By the time she returned, it was late afternoon. She found the book she had purchased in the airport gift shop and went to the patio. It seemed a lot warmer than earlier in the day, but there was still the breeze off the water. Feeling almost fully relaxed in months, she opened the pages of her book and began to read. It wasn't long before the eyes closed and the book fell to her lap.

It took all week, but the unpacking was done. The room was empty with extra boxes and supplies stacked in the closet. She moved the furniture over and finished making the room into a nice guest bedroom. The next big project was to set up her studio. She had thought of nothing else, but knew if she had set it up first, the boxes would still be waiting to get unpacked. Anxiously she began to clean and ready her future studio.

She had taken time to walk to town a few times for coffee and dessert, but still hadn't succumbed to the calling of the shops. Tomorrow she would venture into those enticing stores. Tomorrow, she would shop.

Most of her clothes had been given to the thrift store before moving. She went from store to store, looking, trying on and purchasing. She bought several outfits, most of which were typical island dress, full of color. She also purchased a few traditional outfits. A new life not only meant a new city and a new home; it also meant a new look.

The shopping spree didn't stop with clothes, it continued to include shoes, hats, and purses. She glanced at the hand-made jewelry and drooled, but refrained, at least for now. Shopping nonstop all morning, it was time for lunch and some local food. Eleanor found a café on the beach and tried the pot fish and fungi, an island favorite, with rum cake for dessert.

Shopping done and stomach fed; Eleanor started for home. It had never felt that far, but with all the bags, her body and arms were getting tired. Beads of sweat forming on her forehead as she staggered inside the condo. Her arms so numb, the packages dropped one by one, the contents spilling out on the floor. With unsteady legs, she snatched a bottle of water and wobbled to the patio. Collapsing on a lounge chair, she appreciated the breeze and having her feet propped up. The numbness of her arms changed to a slight shaking before finally calming to a gentle ache.

Rubbing her face with the cool water bottle, she would recoup for a while longer and look at all her finds later. Today was fun, but the walk back was almost too much with everything she had to carry. Taxi services would have to be investigated, or maybe a small car.

The more she thought about a car, the more she liked the idea. Having a car would let her not only transport her larger purchases, but also let her see the island. She hadn't really been anywhere except the beach and the town. According to the brochures, the island had a lot to offer. There were several tours she could take, but she didn't want to have someone dictate her time spent at each location. The more she thought about it, the more she wanted a car.

Relaxed and refreshed, Eleanor took the bags to the bedroom. *The island sure has a way of helping me make a new life for myself. At least that is a good excuse for all my purchases.*

She looked at all the tags and realized she had spent quite a bit. *It's good to have new things and it makes me feel like I belong here. I'll have to wear one of my new swimsuits tomorrow when I go to the beach.*

Still restless, Eleanor started working on her studio. She was anxious to paint again, and the sooner the studio was unpacked, the sooner she could start. It was late afternoon, but the energy continued. She stood in the doorway of the room and smiled as she began to strategically plan in her mind where each item should be.

Her easel and paint would go by the patio doors so it would be easier to move in and out. It would also give the best options for lighting. Her kiln could actually go on the patio, as long as she could keep it protected from any adverse weather. She had drying racks that could either go in the shower or against one of the walls. Eleanor didn't bring her art desk, but eyeing the two nightstands sparked an idea of putting a top on them, at least for now. Her drawing table had been taken apart for the move and she was not looking forward to assembling it, so into the closet it went, for now.

Eleanor worked several hours on her studio getting much of it unpacked and placed where she wanted it. Her energy was beginning to dwindle and her stomach was demanding attention. It was time to rustle up something to eat. Fruit salad in hand, she made her way to her favorite dining spot in the house, the patio. This was beginning to be the go to place whether to eat, relax, read, or just about anything else.

She thought about Christmas being less than two weeks away. The stores and restaurants were all decorated, as were many of the condos she saw on her daily beach walks. She had no one to shop for this Christmas and she just treated herself to a brand-new wardrobe, but still she wanted and needed to do something. *Maybe I should put up a tree or unpack the box marked Christmas.*

Eleanor had kept a few favorite Christmas items. It would be the first Christmas without Logan. He loved the holidays and all the baking, gift-giving, and hectic events that went with it. It would also be the first Christmas without Ellery, her only child, and David, who was a wonderful, loving husband and father, and then of course, Madison, her granddaughter that she adored. Yes, Christmas will be different, but she would still rejoice in celebrating her Savior's birth.

Eleanor found the box marked Christmas. She held each ornament with care and allowed her memories to take her back to those precious times. She knew when she got each one and where it hung on the tree. She found a few other decorations tucked in the box she cherished, as well. She remembered the people, the parties, and the laughter. Her mind went to Logan, his love of Christmas, and how he made the holiday special. Christmas had always been a time for joy. *Maybe I should have kept my tree and decorations. I need a tree. I hope they sell trees in town. Amaya will know where to get one.*

"Good morning, Amaya. This is Eleanor Morgan."

"Eleanor. It's good to hear from you. Are you getting settled?" Amaya responded.

"Yes, I am, but I still have some personal touches to do. I wanted to get more into the Christmas spirit, but I got rid of my tree before the move. Is there any place to get a tree, artificial or real?"

"Yes, but I don't think anyone delivers. Do you have a car yet?" Amaya asked.

"Unfortunately, I haven't gotten that far. I was hoping to wait until after Christmas."

"No worries. This is a slow time for me. Would you want to go, say in an hour?" Amaya asked "We could even have lunch while we're out."

"If you don't mind, I'd really appreciate it. An hour is perfect and lunch is my treat."

Laughing, Amaya answered, "See you in an hour."

Amaya arrived right on time and the two women set out to find a Christmas tree. They drove for about fifteen minutes until they came to a larger city.

"There are plenty of places here to get you a tree. We can check out the mall for an artificial tree or there is a tree lot a few blocks from the mall." Amaya announced.

"I love real trees, but an artificial one is more practical for me. I need decorations, too." Eleanor added.

Amaya pulled into a parking spot. "Yes, the same store that sells the trees also has a large selection of ornaments, lights and other Christmas decorations."

The store was large and had several varieties and sizes of trees. Eleanor chose a six-foot blue spruce with lights. She and Amaya left the tree at the counter and went to find a few ornaments and garland.

This took a little more time, as there was so much to choose from. Eleanor decided to go with something completely different and selected wide ribbon to go around the tree instead of garland, blue ornaments, baby's breath, and berry sticks. The special ornaments that she brought with her would be displayed somewhere else in the condo.

Tree and ornaments purchased, the ladies headed to a restaurant inside the mall. They had a nice lunch and pleasant conversation. Eleanor missed having someone to talk to and laugh with. The time with Amaya made her realize that she needed to put more of an effort into meeting people.

Amaya helped Eleanor in with her tree and bags. Eleanor gave her a quick tour of the condo. Amaya loved the studio and art desk made from two nightstands and a board. She told her if she ever wanted a better top for her art desk, there was a place in town.

Eleanor mentioned that she may want to sell the bedroom set including the nightstands. She had an art table to replace her makeshift one, but it needed to be put together. Amaya said to let her know when she was ready, and she would post it, as well as, letting other realtors know. She winked and reminded Eleanor that most people move to the island needing furniture.

They said goodbye and wished each other a Merry Christmas. With Christmas only a ten days away, Eleanor fixed herself a cold glass of ice tea and immediately put the tree up. It would go in the corner of the family room so she could enjoy it whether sitting inside or on the patio. She plugged in the lights and stood back to admire it. The blue ornaments and baby's breath, embraced by the ribbon and white lights gave an elegant and peaceful feeling. The tree would keep the Christmas memories of Logan alive.

Eleanor stepped out on the patio to enjoy the rest of a beautiful afternoon. The beach beckoned for her to take a walk, so she put on a pair of capris and grabbed a hat on the way out. It was always nice to walk in the sand and feel the water on her feet. She must have walked for thirty minutes before turning around.

The walk was invigorating and she took pleasure in looking at all the homes decorated for Christmas. By the time Eleanor was back on her patio, she was hot and thirsty. *I should have walked in the water more on the way back. I wouldn't be so hot if I had.*

Eleanor took her food to the patio to enjoy the tree and slight breeze. It was a good feeling to decorate for Christmas, but an emptiness still prevailed. She thought about Ellery, David, and Madison and imagined what they would be doing for Christmas. She remembered last year, the last Christmas as a family. She and Logan got there around eleven and stayed until early evening. She had baked a pie and took sweet potatoes and a casserole while Ellery prepared everything else. Those were good memories; memories of love and laughter. Eleanor prayed that one day, the laughter would return and more memories could be made.

It was time to begin meeting more people in her neighborhood, so she decided to attend the condo street Christmas party. There were nine beachfront condos in her section. She was glad she had already met her next-door neighbors, allowing her to see a few familiar faces at the party. The fault was her own. She had no one to blame but herself, spending so much time putting her house together and taking walks, instead of meeting people.

Tonight, would be the start of, what she hoped, new friendships. The party was at McLean's, two doors down. She arrived to find the house already filled with people. Maria, her neighbor on the right, greeted her as she came through the door.

"Eleanor, how good to see you," Maria yelled from across the room. "Juan and I would like to introduce you to the rest of your neighbors. They are all anxious to meet you."

"That would be nice. I really have wanted to meet everyone." Eleanor said.

Throughout the evening she met everyone. Elian and Nadia Garcia, Anthony and Grace Marsh, Robert and Hannah McLean, and Daniel and Charlotte Rogers, all who lived to the north of her. On the south side of Eleanor's condo were Juan and Maria Melendez, Matt and Nikki Steele and finally, John and Lillian Wheatley.

The party was festive and the food delicious. Eleanor had a wonderful time and went home feeling a sense of belonging. She was sure friendships would be formed and she wouldn't be so alone. It felt good to get back home and take her shoes off. Putting on pajamas and picking up the book she had been reading, Eleanor sat on the patio appreciating, again, her tree and evening breeze. She read late into the night.

With only two days until Christmas, Eleanor was almost ready. Today she would put an order in for delivery. She liked walking into town and picking out what she wanted before it was delivered. Tradition was a turkey dinner, but since it was just her, she chose a chicken. She decided on sweet potatoes, carrots, and squash as the sides, along with fresh baked bread. On the way home, she bought a colorful mix of flowers to create a bouquet for her Christmas table. Eleanor loved flowers and made a note to plant many of them in her garden. Until then, she may have to splurge and pick up fresh flowers whenever she was in town.

Tonight was Christmas Eve. She turned on the television and watched all of her and Logan's favorite Christmas movies until early morning. She drank coffee and did some knitting as she watched the movies, with only the tree lights on. It was a peaceful evening. She continued to miss Logan.

Christmas morning proved to be a glorious day. Not only was it the birth of her Savior, but the sun was shining and the gentle breeze flowed through the house. She turned the tree lights on before starting a small pot of coffee. Christmas presents to herself, in addition to the new wardrobe, consisted of several books, yarn, and a few art supplies. She took her coffee to the patio, soaking in the morning air before making her Christmas dinner. *Wait, I'm not on any time table. I can have Christmas dinner whenever I want. I can take a long walk on the beach and even do a little painting, while everything cooks.*

Walking on the beach was peaceful. She decided everyone must be inside opening gifts or having breakfast. She wasn't even sure how many of her neighbors were home and how many went to share Christmas with loved ones. The walk was good, but she was excited to get back to her studio. She called out "Merry Christmas" to Maria and John, who were sitting on their patio.

Inside, she spent time in the kitchen preparing all the side dishes. She seasoned the chicken the night before so it could go in the oven when the side dishes were ready. Preparation done, she went to the studio and looked at the canvas which had been sitting on the easel for a week. Eleanor hadn't been able to get in the mood to paint, but today, it was time. She moved the easel to the patio and began to paint the beach and sea.

Later, she set the patio table for her Christmas dinner, complete with the bouquet of flowers in the center. The wind had picked up some, but it was still a lovely evening to celebrate Christmas and have dinner outside. She may be alone, but God was still with her. Comforting as that was, tears streamed down her face as she ate. Later, she sat in front of the tree and stared at the television while Christmas movies played.

The entire day was exhausting with all the emotions exploding in her head; not to mention her heart. One moment she was happy and the next she was sad. She loved her new home, the town, and all the people she met; but still missed her old home and family. She had the memories, for which she was glad, but she could no longer physically enjoy them. She prayed each day God would allow her to move forward and the hurt of losing Logan would lessen. She never wanted to forget him, only to be happy once again, without him.

Morning proved to be a rainy day with the wind blowing and the waves crashing against the shore. Even with all the drapes open, the inner rooms of the house were dark enough to require the lights to be on. Eleanor wanted to work on her painting, but the lighting would be so different than yesterday.

Maybe I should change my painting of a clear and calm day on the Caribbean Sea to a stormy one. Much like my life right now. It was something she had never done before as an artist. Eleanor made the decision that it was time to push through her safety net. New life and new challenges.

Chapter 6
A Lonely Christmas

Ellery and Madison were in the kitchen baking cookies for an upcoming party. The last week had been a whirlwind of activities and this week was proving to be about the same. Ellery needed to take cupcakes to Madison's school party and cookies to the church program. David didn't have his office party until the week of Christmas, making it extremely close to finishing last minute things for Christmas dinner and shopping.

David invited his sister, Kristin, her husband and two boys to come for Christmas, so that meant cooking, cleaning, and preparing the guest room. He didn't get to see his sister often and Ellery was glad to have company for the holidays, hoping to fill the void of not having her parents present. They were expected to arrive Christmas Eve, but that was still tentative.

"Mom," Madison said. "Are we freezing all these cookies until my program at church?"

"Most of them. We'll keep a few out to eat. Can't make cookies and not eat some of them." Ellery winked at Madison.

"What do I smell?" David said as he walked into the kitchen.

"Cookies!" Madison yelled out.

"Are they for eating now or later?" He asked.

"Both," Ellery replied. "But leave enough for Madison's church program.

"That's not until next week. I'm sure I'll eat most of them by then, so you'll have to bake more." David gave Ellery a mischievous grin.

"No, dad," Madison said. "You can have a few, but then they go into the freezer until my program."

"Oh, that's not fair," David laughed, snatching one more cookie before leaving the room.

Madison was happy to have her mom all to herself. She always had her dad, but it was only until she got her gramma out of the picture did she feel like her mom belonged to her. Madison hated to share anything, especially her parents. *If Gramma had just stayed away, then Mom would have paid more attention to me, and I wouldn't have had to lie. Mom will get over missing gramma, I'm sure.*

She felt bad for her mom, but just a little. Her mom, she believed, would soon forget about Gramma, and then it would be the three of them forever. Her chat group had been totally behind her and praised her for what she did. They encouraged her whenever she was feeling guilty. She would go in the chat room today and get a boost of encouragement before letting guilt creep in.

A snow storm had finally left enough on the ground to make it feel like Christmas. The outside lights, the Christmas tree in the living room, and the whole house decorated helped build the excitement. The house was buzzing as everyone took part in preparing for their guests.

David's sister had asked about Eleanor, but was only told that she was away. This is what everyone was told who asked if Eleanor was joining them for Christmas. The three made a pack to all say the same thing; she was doing fine, but with Logan's death she needed to get away. It was working perfectly, but the question remained, how long would this story work?

Ellery took off work to be at Madison's school Christmas party. All the students in her class had to bring a gift of less than five dollars. Girls for girls and boys for boys. Madison had carefully wrapped her gift of two bracelets, a jump rope, and some candy. The room was loud with children laughing and singing. Moms standing on the outside, watching the events unfold.

Ellery remembered all the parties her mom came to. The memories tugged at her heart making her miss her even more. She quickly pulled herself out of remembrance lane and concentrated on her daughter, whose happiness at this point, meant everything. Madison caught her mom's attention and held up her gifts; a paint set, tablet, hair ties, and candy.

Of all the gifts for Madison to get, a paint set. Ellery's mother was an artist and spent years painting. The painting in the guest room was done by her mom. She had almost forgotten it was there and was now hoping David would too. She also hoped Kristin wouldn't notice when they came at Christmas and say something. Ellery couldn't bear to part with it. She needed to remove it as soon as she could, and put it in the attic. Another painting could go in its place. She hoped no one would notice the change.

David came home from work and called to Madison. The two of them talked in hushed tones and then disappeared upstairs. A few minutes later they returned with a smug grin that meant they had a secret.

The Sunday before Christmas was the church program. Madison was ready for her small part in one of the choral sections. She loved being on stage and performing and Ellery encouraged her daughter's love for acting. One of her Christmas presents was something Madison had been asking the last several years for, voice lessons. As Ellery heard her sing her short solo, she knew it was the right gift.

"I'm bushed." Ellery said on her way home.

"Me too," replied David. "How about you Madison?"

There was no response. Madison was asleep. Ellery smiled. "Glad there's no school tomorrow. I think I'll let her sleep in."

"Good idea. Can I sleep in, too? Please?" David asked.

"No You have appointments, teeth to tend to, and an office to run." Ellery laughed.

Kristin, John, and their sons, Lucas and Liam, would be arriving Christmas day from Phoenix. Ellery knew after a long flight, especially during the holidays, Kristin and John would be tired, but the boys would be like the ball in a pinball machine; bouncing off of anything and everything. She had instructed Madison to take them to the basement family room and let them play ping-pong or watch television. After they settled down some she could feel free to go to her room. The cousins were all similar in age; Madison had just turned 12, Lucas 11, and Liam 8.

Madison was happy when her dad told her that Aunt Kristin and Uncle John had changed their plans from

Christmas Eve to Christmas Day. She had worked too hard to get her parents to herself, especially on Christmas. She didn't particularly like that they were coming at all during the holiday, but late afternoon on Christmas was better than sharing Christmas Eve and morning. She was willing to compromise, despite the fact they were coming, and have a good time.

She always had fun with her cousins and since they don't get to see snow often, outside sledding and hopefully ice skating would be on the agenda. Since Madison loved both of these activities, it wouldn't be too much of a burden, and besides, she could spare three days. She would have the rest of her break to spend with her parents and maybe even have a sleepover with friends.

The next few days were the busiest of all. Ellery and Madison made sure the house was spotless and the guest room was ready. The basement was also cleaned, as the boys would be camping out in the family room. Ellery was glad she had convinced David to put in a three-quarter bath off the laundry room. She also breathed a sigh of relief that no one had noticed her mom's painting being switched.

Christmas Eve finally arrived, which meant an evening of watching Christmas movies, eating pizza and popcorn. Madison was allowed to stay up until eleven, which she saw as special, but her parents saw as being able to sleep in longer on Christmas morning. Each of them got to choose one movie. Madison always looked forward to this evening. It was just for the three of them.

Christmas morning came all too quickly for David and Ellery, but not for Madison. She was still at an age where it was magical and sleep wasn't needed on this particular morning. Madison ran down the stairs yelling, "Get up! Get up!"

David and Ellery heard their daughter and moaned, as they put their robes on and urged their bodies forward. Sitting around the tree, Madison opened her gifts. She got everything she had asked for, but the one present she didn't expect was voice lessons. Madison squealed in delight, hugging both her parents, and saying thank you over and over. Ellery and David smiled at what this small gift did for their daughter.

Ellery loved everything from David and Madison, and was surprised when she opened the combination sewing and embroidery machine. She loved to sew and wanted to take lessons to learn more techniques. Her mind was already thinking of all the things she could make and then embroider.

David also, loved his gifts, and didn't seem too surprised at the new set of golf clubs. He had been giving multiple hints since Thanksgiving. He was surprised, though, when he opened the card that accompanied the clubs; twelve lessons with the golf pro at the country club they belonged to.

Gifts opened and breakfast done, the three cleaned up the morning mess. Ellery had the turkey set to go in the oven at noon and then made sure everything else was ready. David would always tease her on over planning, but Ellery knew this was the only way to relax and spend time with Kristin and John before having to get food on the table. Madison finished setting the table and joined her dad in front of the television to watch Miracle on 34th Street. It was another Christmas day tradition.

The day seemed to go by slowly, which Ellery was glad for, because the house would soon be filling up with all kinds of energy. She looked at the clock and knew David and Madison would return any minute with their guests. *I do so enjoy my quiet times, and this one is almost gone.* Just as soon as the thought entered her mind, the door opened ending her relished silence. The group piled in, all talking at the same time.

Ellery ran to hug each of them, collecting their coats as they talked. David announced he and John would take the suitcases to the guest room and instructed Madison to take the boys downstairs to the family room

Ellery couldn't stop talking. She was so hungry for someone to talk to and share the holidays with. She told

Kristin to make herself comfortable, as she hung up the coats. "I'll be back in a few minutes with coffee and cake. You just relax."

"Do you need any help?" Kristin asked.

"I can handle it. Take this opportunity to relax. Madison and the boys will be fine in the family room."

"Okay. I am going to take you up on the offer, but know that I will be rested enough to help with dinner." Kristin said.

Dinner was a time for talking, laughing, and catching up on all the news. The adults were happy to stay at the table longer and continue to talk and enjoy another cup of coffee, but they couldn't ignore the pleas from three begging faces.

The food was quickly put away before the exchange of presents. A flurry of wrapping paper soon filled the air. Ellery and Kristin caught each piece as it came down, making sure no gift was being thrown away. The kids were excited with what they got and quickly asked to be excused to go play. It took less than a second for all adults to shout "Yes!" There was a moment of silence before they laughed and decided another slice of pie was in order.

The three days went by quickly and once again David and Madison were on their way to the airport to drop off Kristin, John and the boys. It had been an almost perfect Christmas for everyone. Madison only had to share part of Christmas day with others and she enjoyed having her cousins to go sledding and ice skating with, but wasn't upset when the time came for them to leave.

For David, it was a perfect time because he got to see his sister and brother-in-law. It had been almost two years since they had gotten together and he missed his little sister. Although she loved spending time with Madison and David, and sharing part of Christmas with Kristin and John, it was a difficult time for Ellery not having her parents there. Would David ever realize just how much her heart was longing for her mom? Ellery was grateful that no one noticed or mentioned the guest room painting swap.

A few days after Christmas, Ellery remembered the letters from the law office. She would need to reach out and see what they wanted. She reminded David of the letters and asked when it would be a good time to contact the attorney.

"Let's wait another week. Madison is still on break and my work load is light. I want to spend time with the two of you. Is that okay?" David asked.

"It's fine with me. I think doing some things together would be nice before our hectic lives take over again. I don't want to forget, though." Ellery smiled.

"Put it on your calendar for the week after New Year's." David suggested.

Chapter 7
The Letter

It was a few days before New Year's when there was a knock on the door. Ellery opened the door and saw Pastor Harris standing there.

"Pastor Harris. Hello." Ellery was a bit startled to see him standing there. Her thoughts became jumbled as they began swirling through her mind.

"Hello Ellery. May I come in?" Pastor Harris asked.

"Yes, please do." Ellery opened the door wide allowing him to enter. She led him to the living room. "May I get you a cup of coffee?"

Chuckling, Pastor Harris replied, "No. Thank you. I'm afraid if I have one more cup of coffee today, I won't sleep for a week."

"Does this visit have something to do with my mom? Is something wrong? Is she hurt or ill? Should I call David in?" Ellery asked.

"That may be helpful to have Davide here." Pastor Harris smiled, but couldn't hide the concern on his face.

Ellery was now becoming worried and anxious. Had something happened to her mom? She went to the basement steps and asked David to come up to meet with Pastor Harris. David came up the stairs with a confused look on his face.

He immediately started getting worked up, but spoke in hushed tones to Ellery. "Pastor Harris is Eleanor's pastor, not ours, so why is he visiting us? Maybe Eleanor told him why we kicked her out of our lives and he wants to have us welcome her back. Well, that's not going to happen."

"David. What if it's because something happened to my mom? Let's just go in and find out before you get angry," Ellery stated.

'Pastor Harris. It's good to see you." David greeted.

"Hello David. It's good to see you also." Pastor Harris said in return.

"So, why the visit?" David got right to the point. Ellery cringed, knowing that David could get very defensive when it came to the topic of her mom.

The pastor started to explain. "I haven't heard from your mother in several weeks. Lisa and I thought she was busy finding a new place to live and maybe just needed some time to get settled, but she hasn't contacted us in quite some time.

David rudely interrupted, "I'm sure she has been very busy and it's nothing."

"That's what we thought at first." Pastor Harris quietly continued, but noted David's annoyance. "So, we stopped in to check on her and ask if she made a decision on where to move to. A stranger answered the door. They said they bought the house and moved in around Thanksgiving."

Ellery felt a chill go down her back. "Maybe you are mistaken, pastor."

"I checked with a few neighbors and they said there was never a sale sign in the yard only a moving van. A few neighbors still saw her the day after the moving van was there, but then she was gone and a new family moved in." Pastor Harris finished by providing the information he had learned. "I had promised Eleanor to keep her plans of moving confidential, but this is out of character for her.

Ellery looked at David, her face ashen. "We haven't seen her. We had… we... that is…"

David was frustrated that Ellery was having trouble with an explanation. "We haven't seen Eleanor either. As you already know, we are not on the best of speaking terms with her." He gave Ellery a warning glance that she needed to get-it-together, and fast..

"Yes, I remember there being some tension between all of you. It still is rather odd that she hasn't let me know where she moved to." Pastor Harris now realized he was in the middle of a rattlesnake's den as he watched Ellery's reaction and the awkward non-verbal interchange between husband and wife.

Pastor Harris cleared his throat. "Well, I must be going. Thank you for putting my mind somewhat at ease. But, please, let me know when you hear from her or if you need anything. I will, in turn, let you know if I hear from her. I want to keep in touch."

Ellery needed to ask, "Mom said she was moving?"

"She didn't want anyone to know, but said she would keep in touch. Lisa and I haven't heard anything from her. Not even a postcard. So, please, let me know if you hear from her. Okay?" The pastor gently touched Ellery's arm, letting her know he would be there if she needed him.

"We will do that, pastor. She must have not wanted us to change her mind. That house held years of memories that she and Logan spent together. It's no wonder she would want to start fresh and not want us to talk her out of moving. I'm sure she'll let us know soon." David briskly walked Pastor Harris to the door.

The door had barely closed before Ellery went into hysterics. "David! My mom. Where is she? I don't even know if she's safe." Her eyes were wide with fear, her hands trembling, as she looked to David to assure her everything would be alright, that her mom was safe.

David provided no such comfort but instead, became aggravated. "She is out of our lives, so what's the big deal? None of us wanted anything to do with her, so now it will be easier. We can tell everyone she moved. If we have to, we'll make up a city she moved to."

Ellery thought she had seen all of David's sides, but this was new. David believed Madison one hundred percent and became protective of her. He had no feelings or even love left for her mom. This put Ellery in a precarious spot. She loved her mom and wanted to see her, but now there may be no chance of accidentally running into her at the mall or an event. She also loved David and Madison and didn't want all of this to build a wall between them. David went back to the family room to finish playing a game with Madison.

She stood in the living room alone and feeling deserted. She couldn't find enough air in the house to breathe. She had to get away for a while. She needed to be completely alone without David and Madison making comments about how happy they were the way this had turned out.

Ellery called down to David and said she needed to get a few things at the store and would be back in about an hour. David reminded her to get more snacks for tonight. She could hardly get the words out, but managed to tell him she would pick up the snacks.

Tears ran down her face as she drove. At times she could hardly see the road. She pulled into the store's parking lot and took a spot far away from the door. She sat there, while her body shook and her heart shattered. *What am I going to do and how will I keep this charade up? I don't want to keep pretending everything is great. Now, David wants me to let people think my mom simply moved away.*

Ellery made a decision as she sat there, that would go against everything David and Madison wanted. She was going to search for her mom; alone. She didn't want to deceive David, but there was no other way. She didn't want to drag Pastor Harris into the mess, either. So, for now, she would secretly search.

She had used up most of her time, so she dried her eyes and put fresh makeup on before going into the store in search of snacks and anything else that would make her trip believable. The air was cool with a slight wind, which helped disguise her red face as being nothing more than weather related.

Tomorrow, after she had time to clearly think things over, she would make a mental list of where to start. She was reluctant to write anything down for fear David or Madison would find it.

The next day, Ellery had time to start thinking of ways to find her mom. Madison was spending the day at a friend's house and David was having lunch with a few college football buddies. She was glad for the time alone, without interruptions or having to hide what she was planning. She remembered Pastor Harris said he talked to the new owners of the house and some of the neighbors, but no one knew anything. She wasn't sure they would have any more information to offer her. *How did mom sell her house, with a realtor or somehow on her own? I wonder if a neighbor remembers the name of the moving company?*

Suddenly she remembered the phone call from her mom and the message she left, 'I love you'. Ellery gasped. *She was saying goodbye! When no one picked up, she left the only message she could, 'I love you'. Mom wouldn't have disrespected our wish for no communication, but she wanted to try one last time before she literally walked out of our lives. She left because of us. She left the home she had shared with Dad for so many years. She walked away from years of precious memories, because ... we ...I... forced her ...out of ...my ...life.*

The pain in her heart was almost too much. A thick, heavy net had been thrown over her. She struggled against the net all day as she made the bed, started a load of wash, and went through her daily routine. All day she fought to get out of the net, but it only seemed to get heavier. *How will I explain my feelings to David and make him understand that I need to find my mom? Will Madison's heart soften or will her heart stay like David's, cold? David continues to believe my mom is some sort of evil that lurks in every corner.*

A few days had passed since the visit from Pastor Harris, when David came home and suggested he and Ellery go out to eat. She wasn't up to eating out, but maybe it would be best to have her mind on something else. Ellery wanted to talk to David about her mom's disappearance and about the last call to them, but the restaurant wasn't the place to do it. She would have to wait until they got home, and hopefully she would still have the courage.

David was relaxed and talkative all through dinner and Ellery worked at giving him all of her attention. She didn't want to ruin his evening and she definitely didn't want him to suspect anything.

They had been home for nearly an hour before Ellery had the nerve to ask if she could talk over something serious with him. He put the book down. "I'm all yours."

"David, please let me get everything out before you respond, okay?" Ellery asked.

"Okay," he said.

"I'm worried about my mother, and I miss her terribly… but mostly… I'm worried. I couldn't think clearly when

Pastor Harris told us he was concerned that she had left town for good. Today, I remembered when she called, and we listened to her message; which was simply 'I love you'. I think she was hoping to tell us she was moving and where she was moving to. David, I want to try and find her."

David looked at Ellery, his anger began to surface. "Absolutely not! I don't want anything to do with your mother and I don't want her worming her way back into our lives. I won't stop you from looking for her, for your peace of mind, but only to learn where she is and that she is okay. You are not to make any contact. Is that clear?"

"David. She's my mother. What would happen if someone told Madison she could never talk to me or see me again? Would you want that for your daughter?" Ellery's voice quivered.

David was annoyed, but kept his anger under control. "Ellery, we're not talking about you and Madison. We're talking about your mother who abused our daughter, or have you forgotten? Now, I think my offer is more than fair to put your mind at ease. You can either accept that offer or not."

She looked at her husband and finally realized he had allowed his heart to become calloused where her mom was concerned.

Neither one heard the back door open. Madison had come home early and was standing quietly in the kitchen listening to her parents talk about Gramma. *Had Gramma really sold the house and moved away?* Hearing her mom's comment about how she would feel if someone told her she could never talk to her daughter again, was like getting hit in the face with a snowball. She heard the pain in her mom's voice and the hardness in her dad's.

Did I go too far in order to get my own way and in order to have Mom and Dad all to myself? Had Gramma told Grampa what I was doing all the time? What did he think of me before he died? Did I cause his heart attack?

It was quiet in the living room. Madison opened the back door and shut it loudly so they would know she was home. She didn't want them to know she had overheard their conversation. "Hi Mom. Hi Dad. I'm home."

"Hi sweetheart," her dad called out.

"Did you have a good time today?" Ellery squashed her personal anguish in order to be attentive to her daughter.

"Yes. We went roller skating." Madison replied.

"That sounds like fun. Did you eat or are you hungry? Mom and I went out to eat, but I'm sure we can find something in the kitchen or I can order a pizza and we can all watch a movie. What do you want?"

Madison couldn't look at her mom, but didn't hesitate to answer. "I would love pizza and a movie, if that's okay with Mom."

"It sounds like a great idea, although, I'm not really hungry yet, but I can always eat some later, unless you and your dad eat it all first." Ellery said, trying to sound upbeat.

"I'll order the pizza in about ten minutes. That gives everyone time to get comfy clothes on. You ladies decide on a movie when I go for the pizza, okay?"

"Okay. Dad, Mom, any requests?" Madison asked.

Ellery and David shook their heads, so it was up to Madison for the final say.

Movie night was different than most. Madison had chosen a comedy to watch, but there was little laughter in the room. They all smiled and forced a laugh here and there to make each other think nothing was wrong. David was disappointed that his wife wanted to find Eleanor after what she did to Madison. It was Eleanor's doing that the communication was broken, not his. Madison was feeling sorry for her mom, but at the same time her head would not let her fully regret what she had done. She liked having her parents to herself. Ellery was dealing with so many emotions from missing her mom and wanting to find her, to confusion over her husband's attitude, to Madison's apathetic stance on her gramma.

93

David and Ellery sat waiting for the attorney to enter. David believed that Eleanor was behind this meeting and came prepared for a fight. Ellery nervously awaited, hoping that it wasn't her mom's doing. Jake Townsend came in and greeted them.

Jake took his seat at the table. "Ellery, first let me extend my condolences. Your father was not only a client, but a friend. I have already met with your mother regarding the trust they had and also a separate account." Ellery could feel David's body tightening. She prayed he would allow Mr. Townsend to finish. "Separate from your parents trust, your father had two other accounts. As I stated, one account was for your mom, but the second account was for you. Your dad also left you a letter."

She gasped. *Dad left me a letter?* Looking at David and then at the attorney. "A letter? When did he write it?"

"He wrote it about four months before his passing. I will give you the letter so you can read it in private. However, I would like to go over the savings account your father also left you, now.

Ellery nodded, as she took David's hand. David squeezed her hand, letting her know everything will be okay. Jake turned the files for them to see.

"Your father opened two accounts separate from the trust. As I said, one account for your mom and the other for you. As you can see here, it is quite a substantial amount. A little over one hundred thousand. You have a few options; keep it in this account and have it continue earning interest, transfer to an account or stock of your choosing, or cash it out." Jake finished to give them time to think about the options.

"I had no idea that Dad had anything other than a living trust. I'm not sure what to do. How soon do we need to make a decision? I know David and I would like some time to talk about this." Ellery stated.

Jake took a moment to reassure them. "You don't have to make a decision today. In fact, you can make changes at any time, even a year from now. I do need you to acknowledge, by signature, that you have been made aware of this and all options have been explained to you."

"Honey. Sign the acknowledgement and then we can take our time before deciding. While we decide, the money will continue to stay invested and grow." David said.

Ellery and David left the office. She held the letter from her father to her chest, caressing the envelope for several minutes, David finally asked, "Are going to open it before you shred it with your fingers?"

"I'm sorry. I just can't believe Dad wrote me a letter, knowing he may have little time left. Yet, he couldn't bear to tell me in person." Ellery said.

"You won't know anything if you don't read it." David took a deep breath and asked her, "Do you want me to read it or maybe you would prefer to be alone to read it?"

"No. I can read it, but I want you here. I need you here." Ellery stammered. "This has all been a shock to me. First that dad had a separate savings account just for me – really for us. Then a personal letter. He was always so thoughtful and planning for the future. I just never realized how much he planned. How much he planned for me."

"Your dad was one of a kind. A strong but gentle man. He was the best. He treated me like a son. I loved him as much as my own dad." David said.

"My dearest Ellery,

I have been so proud to be your Dad. I know you are wondering why I didn't tell you of my heart condition. I wanted a normal life. I wanted laughter and smiles. I didn't want to be a burden or be pitied. I'm sure your mom explained my wishes to you, and I trust you can understand and even forgive me for not saying anything. Your mother wasn't in total agreement of keeping this from you and David, but I insisted.

Please tell David that, as far as I am concerned, he is my son. I love that he loves you, as I love your mother.

He has taken good care of you and I know he always will. David, continue to be the rock of the family.

Mom is going to need all of you to lean on. She says she is prepared, but that is what she needs to cling to. Her heart will be broken, so please help her heal.

Let Madison know that she is the jewel of the family. She is smart, funny, and very athletic. Takes after me, I suppose. She will do well. Keep her safe for me and let her spread her wings. I will remember her smile and her love, always.

Love Dad

Ellery closed the letter and buried her head into David's shoulder. "Mom was telling us the truth. It was Dad's decision to keep it from all of us. I said some awful and hurtful things to her, and now she's gone. Maybe forever. Will Dad ever forgive me? Will Mom ever forgive me?"

David was silent. *I was wrong about Eleanor on this, but I still believe my daughter. Eleanor may receive my forgiveness on this, but not where Madison is concerned. She abused her and for that, nothing changes.* But his heart softened as he held his wife. *I will support her search, but I will not help her search. If she finds Eleanor, I will deal with that then.*

Chapter 8
A New Life

Eleanor spent many days painting either in the studio or on the patio. When touring the island, she would take a canvas or sketch pad with her; but found it too cumbersome. She decided a camera was needed and took time to about them and photography before purchasing the one she thought would be best for her. Using a camera would allow her to capture the scene in real time and paint later.

She took a few classes in photography and found she enjoyed it. She spent hours traveling and walking the beaches, while photographing everything she could from different angles. After a few weeks, she examined each photo with a critical eye and sent some off to be enlarged, even framing a few of them.

Several people that came to the house admired the art work on the walls and inquired about the artists. Surprised to find that she was both the artist and photographer, asked if she sold any of her works. Eleanor explained it was really just a hobby and hadn't thought about selling them. Her friends all told her that her work was more than a hobby – it was amazing and should be in a gallery.

She knew her artistic abilities were good enough to teach or paint for her family, but she never thought of herself as someone who could sell her work; let alone her photographs. Eleanor thought about what people said and decided to take a risk. She found an art gallery in town and checked it out.

The owner of the gallery looked at each piece Eleanor brought in and was pleased with her work. She offered to show both her paintings and photography on a consignment basis. The gallery took forty percent and Eleanor received the remaining sixty percent. Even though it meant giving up some of the profits, it was a start to see if anyone would purchase her work. Eleanor left her art pieces at the gallery and headed for home. Her mind was now reeling with ideas and questions about doing more to show her work. *My friends mentioned posting my work online and even having an online store. I have no idea how to do it, but I know someone who does.*

Mateo, her next-door neighbor's son, volunteered to create several social media platforms for her. Eleanor was familiar with social media, but had no idea how to create a site, let alone show and sell her work. When he was done she was amazed and very impressed at how great the sites looked. Within a few short weeks she had what he called, hits and likes.

Around the same time, Dalila, from the art gallery, called and said there had been some interest in two of her paintings and one of her photographs. After describing the pieces that received the interest, she surprised Eleanor by saying one had been sold. Eleanor was shocked. She thought her work might get a few people to look and comment on, but never thought any of it would sell, at least this quickly. Eleanor hung up the phone and smiled, feeling like a child with a brand new toy.

Eleanor received another surprising call later in the week. The local Christian school was interested in having her teach art classes twice a week for grades four through six. It had been a long time since she had been in a classroom and she was hesitant and a little nervous to make such a commitment. After thinking it over for a few days, she called the school and said yes. Classes started in three weeks and the principal told her to come in any time to set up the classroom and inventory the supplies.

The classroom was small, but the wall of windows let in a great deal of light. The room had enough tables and stools for the students on her roster. The wall opposite the windows was lined with a long counter and an abundance of cupboards, and the back wall had a large sink with hooks for art smocks. There was also a good size closet for extra storage. She would share her room with another teacher that taught art for kindergarten through third grade.

In the last year, Eleanor had stepped out and embraced her new life. She joined a book club, taken a flower arranging class, and found a church family. She was out in the community, meeting people, working, and volunteering. She met several of the neighbors for walks on the beach and joined in the cookouts. Eleanor enjoyed her neighbors and all the activities, but it wasn't the same as family. She missed her family so much that a day didn't go by where her heart didn't ache to hold them. She talked with friends about Logan and their wonderful life together. She told them about Ellery, her beautiful daughter, David her wonderful son-in-law, and Madison and what an amazing granddaughter she was. She held close to her heart, though, the secret that they were estranged. Even with the absence of family, Eleanor knew she was home.

Alienated from her family didn't stop Eleanor from communicating in her own way. Every week, usually on

Sunday, she sat down and wrote a long letter to her daughter. She started this ritual a week after she moved, as a way to help her cope with the loss. She would write about everything she did during the week, describing the scenery and weather, who she met, what she painted, and what she took pictures of. She included several photos and often times a watercolor. She found the writing not only therapeutic, but in a way, allowed her to feel closer to her daughter.

Art classes at the school were in full swing and Eleanor was happy to see children expressing themselves in so many ways. The doubts and fears that she had been out of the classroom too long, faded away. Her art colleague, Susan, was fantastic. She was young and energetic and had so many new ideas for teaching art. They worked out the progression of skills, division of supplies, and displaying art work. Susan, had even suggested doing an art fair in the spring.

Eleanor began thinking about traveling again. She and Logan had always wanted to travel. They had dreamed of an Alaskan cruise. She spent many hours at the travel agency looking at all of her the options. She looked through all the books on the different cruises and places to go. *This is such a hard decision. I want the Alaskan cruise, but I also want to go to Denali, and going through Canada looks amazing. I'm afraid to see the prices of all of these trips. Maybe if I save all of my teaching salary, I could somehow afford to do all three. It may take a while to save, but is it possible?* The travel agent put together several packages for her to think about and suggested she make the arrangements six to nine months in advance.

The second Thanksgiving in her new home was fast approaching, as Eleanor continued to keep as busy as she could. Several neighbors, with no family near, planned to have Thanksgiving dinner together, which she volunteered to host. Each family would pitch in bringing food, beverages, and, most importantly, desserts. Eleanor said she would cook the turkey if someone else could bring the ham. She was beginning to look forward to a traditional Caribbean Thanksgiving.

The aromas that came from Eleanor's house that day filled the air making your mouth water and your stomach begging to eat. Mendo brought grilled snapper with Caribbean green seasoning and Lillian came with mashed rutabagas and sweet potato stuffing with raisins. There was honey-glazed ham and Caribbean red beans and rice. Eleanor tried her hand, with the guidance of Nadia, to make Pavochon, a Puerto Rican roast turkey. The desserts were amazing, and included; Besitos de Coco, Bacardi rum-soaked cake, Ensaimada Mallorquina (a spiral pastry), and Hummingbird cake with cream cheese frosting.

Throughout the day there was much eating, talking,

laughing, walking on the beach, and watching the children play games. The evening came to an end and Eleanor found herself alone. She was tired, but with a peaceful and grateful heart.

Only three weeks until Christmas and Eleanor found herself busier than she could ever remember. There was the school Christmas program that she and Susan had volunteered to paint the backgrounds for. The church program needed some art work done, and she volunteered to supervise two high school art students doing most of the work. The condo community had organized a Christmas party and suggested they draw names for Secret Santa. Eleanor drew Charlotte's name and began to work on screen printing a scarf for her.

She had been invited to spend Christmas day with Pastor Tony, his wife Juanita, and their four children ranging in ages from two to fifteen. She secretly photographed each child and then all four together as a gift for the pastor and his wife.

For the second year, Eleanor put her tree up, alone. She sat each evening watching Christmas movies and knitting. The tree was a comfort, wrapping its branches around her, keeping her warm and loved. The lights reminded her of God's love and how He has taken care of her through all the heartache of the past few years. The lights were shining the way to a new life. It was not a better life, just new.

Christmas Eve was peaceful. The Christmas lights from nearby homes shone off the water. A large ship was in the distant and the lights seemed to shout "Merry Christmas" to her as it passed by. Eleanor wrapped an afghan around her as a cool breeze flowed into the room. Content she sat sipping her tea and watching a favorite movie. Tonight, she was at peace.

Christmas day was finally here and she had never witnessed so much energy and noise from one family. In addition to the pastor's family and herself, they were joined by Juanita's parents, her five siblings, and the their families. The pastor's older sister and family, plus several aunts and uncles rounded out the celebration. The amount of food was triple what she had at Thanksgiving and the desserts never seemed to end. Children were running in and out, wrapping paper littering the floor, and everyone was so happy to be together. It was almost too much for Eleanor to watch, although she appreciated the invitation. She needed to leave before her emotions were unwrapped and displayed for all to see. She thanked her hosts for a wonderful time, wished everyone a Merry Christmas, and headed home.

A walk on the beach with the breeze and sea spray hitting her felt refreshing. Today she really missed Logan with his smile and laugh. She missed his warmth and tenderness. She thought about Ellery, David, and Madison.

Were they well and happy or did they still despise her? This was to be a day of celebration and happiness, and yet it had turned into a day of heartbreaking memories and impossible wishes. Back home, she sat on the lounge chair and wept. Exhausted from all the emotions, sleep forced its way on her.

When she awoke the sky was grey and threatening, and the gentle breeze was turning into a strong wind. It looked like an intense storm was fast approaching. People were hurrying off the beach, hoping to reach shelter before the skies opened. Eleanor folded up the lounge chairs and laid them down, along with the table chairs. She brought in all the cushions and small items that could sprout wings. Looking at the sky getting darker and darker by the minute, she stepped inside and closed the windows facing the beach. She kept the family room patio doors open for now, but knew, they too, would have to be closed.

It was a turbulent storm, the sea swelled as if it were alive, bulging with churning grey water. The storm was unlike anything Eleanor had witnessed before. She found her flashlight in case the power went out, made some coffee, and warmed up the leftovers Juanita had sent home with her. Making herself comfortable, she watched as the wind and waves all fought against each other. She had two options, reading or painting, to keep herself occupied. The storm seemed to sit over her house for the next hour. The lights flickered a few times, but never completely went off. Eleanor was relaxed and calm as she painted the furry around her.

The storm finally quieted even though the rain continued. She was amazed at how fast she finished the painting. It usually took her a few days, but tonight, her brushes seemed to float quickly over the canvas. The storm outside and the storm inside combined forces and made it onto the canvas. Eleanor cleaned her brushes and put away the paints before she settled in her favorite chair to read.

It was a different and somewhat strange Christmas day, filled first with sunshine, happiness, and laughter, before turning into sadness, loneliness, and darkness. Tomorrow the sun will shine, again.

Chapter 9
Still No Trace

Ellery wasn't getting anywhere trying to find out information about her mom. She confided in Pastor Harris and Lisa about the accusations and how adamant David was to never communicate with her again. She was confused why David wouldn't even hear her mom's side of the story, and why now that she's missing, doesn't care whether they find her or not. It was a long session, but Ellery felt better for having told someone the truth.

Pastor Harris and Lisa said they still hadn't heard from Eleanor, but would let her know if and when they do. The visit would be kept confidential and they told Ellery to call anytime. Before she left the three prayed for a peaceful heart and that Eleanor would be found safe and healthy.

Logan's sister and family came for Thanksgiving. The days were filled with baking, shopping, games, and laughter. It was good for Ellery to have something to take up her time instead of being alone with her thoughts. The time passed quickly and Christmas was only a few weeks away. Ellery's list of what had to be done before December 25 was long, but feasible. She had the standard parties to prepare for and attend, last minute shopping, and gift wrapping. Madison's school and church parties were only a few days apart this year, so freezing the baked goods wouldn't be necessary.

Christmas day would be quieter than last year with only the three of them. Logan's college friend was coming in the late afternoon to visit for a few hours on his way through town. Madison was very happy that this Christmas she didn't have to share her parents with anyone. She didn't consider the short visit from her dad's college friend an interference.

David and Ellery both noticed that Madison was in exceptionally high spirits and seemed to be happier this Christmas. They didn't question it. She was happy and that's all that mattered. Madison may be happier and more content, but Ellery continued to be on a roller coaster of emotions, which stalled at the bottom of the hill and struggled each time to reach the top.

Ellery suddenly turned her attention to a weather bulletin streaming across the television. A winter storm was predicted to hit the area on Christmas Eve and continue through Christmas day making travel very difficult. A last-minute dash to the store to stock up on batteries, candles, and such was called for. They knew what a severe snow storm meant. David and Ellery chose a book while Madison chose a few activities to do.

"Best be prepared," David said.

"Yes. It's always a good excuse to eat junk and read." Ellery offered.

Christmas Eve proved the weatherman correct. A gentle rush of flurries started late afternoon and by midnight the winds had picked up substantially. The snow kept falling faster and faster. It looked like the snowflakes were fighting each other for space and drifts were competing to form the highest peak, like shifting sands in a desert.

Christmas morning the weather looked no better; in fact, it was much worse with violent winds howling loudly. They opened their gifts, listening to screams from Madison as she unwrapped each one. Retiring to the living room, David turned on the television in time to see the weather report. The forecasted severe snowstorm had turned into a Christmas Day blizzard.

"I'm glad we don't have to travel or have any loved ones traveling," David said. "I don't expect Doug to make it over today either, but I'll call and find out for sure. He's crazy if he thinks of traveling anywhere today." The weatherman went on to talk about all of the power outages and more to come. A few minutes later, the lights flickered and the power went out.

"I have flashlights when it gets darker and I'll put candles out." Ellery said. "David, I forgot to check the wood supply for the fireplace. We might want to start it before it gets too cold in here."

"Beat you to it. I brought wood inside the garage yesterday and filled up the wood bin by the fireplace. I'll get one started now."

"Madison," Ellery said. "Why don't you get some warm clothes and blankets. Also, maybe some things to do. Get the comforter off my bed. I'll get warm clothes for Dad and I when I'm done in the kitchen."

"Okay, Mom." Madison said as she ran upstairs.

David shut the French doors to the foyer in order to keep the heat centralized. He didn't want to have the heat from the fireplace warming up unnecessary areas. Ellery filled a few storage containers with snacks and put ice in the cooler for drinks. She changed into her sweats, got out some thick socks, and grabbed her robe and slippers. She would make sure David did the same, as she knew from experience that these blizzards could last a few days and chances of getting electricity back before then were slim.

Ellery heard Madison as she came down, "Did you also get warm socks, a robe and slippers?"

"I'll go get them now. I couldn't carry everything, Mom." Madison laughed. "Do we need more blankets?"

"I think we're fine, but I'll get a few more from the guest room, just in case. You just get what you need."

Everything they needed was now in the living room and a warm fire was already going. They had learned it was easier to keep the house warm if you started the fire early. David was concerned that he didn't have enough wood, so he went back outside and brought more into the garage to start drying.

"I'm glad I went with my gut and cooked the turkey and a few side dishes last night." Ellery said. "I was afraid the power would go out and we would sit with an uncooked turkey. We can at least make turkey sandwiches or warm up food in the fireplace … maybe."

They were prepared to start playing a game when Ellery blurted out, "David, what if we took the turkey and other items, put them in the those extra bins with tops, and stick them in the garage to keep cold?"

"The garage is like a refrigerator. It's worth a try." David answered. "Madison, help Mom while I get the bins."

"Okay. Then can we play a game before it gets too dark?" Madison asked.

"Agreed. By the way, I bought several lanterns and enough oil to get us through all of this; giving us enough light to play games and read."

Everyone laughed and gave David a high-five.

A snowy war had been waged on the city. Throughout the night they listened to nature's revenge from screeching winds. The gentle flakes of snow had turned to ice and the large frozen pellets struck the windows with the force of missiles. It was as if the world stopped. The clocks stopped telling time. There was no communication from the outside world. Everything was dark, except for the angry white confetti swirling around the house, calling for the occupants to surrender.

Daylight gave way to the destruction from the storm during the night. Tree limbs had been decapitated from the trunk and their front hedges were flattened from the heavy snow. The already frigid temperatures were continuing to fall. A complete whiteout from ground to sky. Looking out the window, David said, "I once heard a weatherman define a blizzard as a snowstorm on steroids."

Madison joined her parents at the window. "It looks like we're inside a giant snow globe that's constantly being shaken. Will it ever stop?"

"Eventually, Madison. Eventually." David murmured.

The blizzard continued throughout the second night and most of the next day before winding down. They had been blessed to have the right weapons to defend against the storm; a fireplace and enough food and drink to last several days.

During the storm, Ellery took time to write down her thoughts while the two were reading or napping. She started a journal to capture everything from when her mom was banished from their lives to now, and even her recent online searches. She was hoping this would serve as therapy and help her conquer the bouts of depression. *I need a heavier sweater. It's also time to stop writing and put this away.*

"What are you doing in here, Ellery? It's way too cold." David asked.

"I'm getting a warmer sweater. Are you okay, or do you need some warmer clothing?" Ellery selected a thick sweater and then closed the drawer. She didn't tell David that she was also hiding her journal.

"As a matter of fact, I could use a heavier sweater." David went to his dresser and searched for one.

That was too close. I have no idea how David would react if he knew my true feelings and that I still question his decision to keep Mom from me.

It took two days after the storm ended before power was restored. Phones charged, food back in the refrigerator, candles and flashlights put away, the family settled back to an almost normal routine. It was still too cold to be outside for any length of time, so board games and movies continued.

David was able to contact his staff and let them know the office would still be closed until the secondary roads opened up. He would try to make it in tomorrow and let them know when they would open the office again.

Madison, like the others, had cabin fever. She was tired of reading, playing games, and being cooped up. She was happier now that the power was back on and didn't have to stay in one room. She spent time in her bedroom rearranging posters and doing some painting. Madison showed promise as an artist, which made Ellery miss her mom even more.

Ellery continued to write in her journal each day. The return of power, gave her time to continue the search for her mom, but only when David and Madison were out of the house. She was becoming frustrated at not getting further in her search, but reminded herself that this was the beginning and patience was needed. *How long will it take before I find something out?*

It had taken the city a long time to get back to normal after the intense blizzard, but the roads were clear for travel. The temperature was now warm enough to allow some outside activities, allowing Madison to go sledding with Angela. Neighbors were busy helping each other dig out from several days of pounding snow and fierce winds.

Madison was glad she still had a few days of her Christmas vacation left. Her friend was having a New Year's Eve party, which she was excited to attend. David and Ellery were also going out with some friends for dinner and then back to their house to welcome the new year in. Ellery was praying that the new year would bring her luck in finding her mom and that they would be reunited.

Ellery had spent every possible free moment searching for the last several months. A few possibilities surfaced, but the details didn't match. Either Scotty beamed her up to the Enterprise or she fell down the rabbit hole with Alice. Most people would rush to file a missing person report, but Eleanor had simply moved, with no notice and no warning. She wasn't really a missing person, it was just that details of her whereabouts were missing.

Today Ellery abandoned the Internet search and began checking all the hospitals and morgues within one hundred miles. Suddenly becoming chilled at the thought of her mom lying in a hospital, hurt or sick, or the unthinkable, a morgue. It was time to try something else. Something she had thought about doing, but allowed the train of time to continue moving down the track because she was afraid to get on.

With unsteady fingers, she dialed the number. *What do I do if she answers? I can't give her any hope and David made it more than perfectly clear I was to have no contact.*

The ringing stopped and someone she didn't know answered it. She apologized and hung up. *Did Mom leave any trace of where she went? Was she so determined to have no one find her that she even changed her phone number?*

Another month went by and still no sign of where her mom could have gone. The panic thermometer was continuing to rise. She had searched methodically within a one-hundred-mile radius but knew it was time to expand the search. *I'm sure my mom didn't leave the country. She wouldn't want to be that far from us, even if we had cut her out of our lives.* But, maybe *she did leave the country, She would have gone south to get away from the winter. That's absurd! No way would she leave the country. She's in the states, but where?*

She started searching nearby states, hoping for any hints of where her mom might be. She continued with the same plan, searching the Internet then looking at all the major cities and surrounding suburbs. She couldn't picture her mom living in a rural area and certainly not off the grid, but couldn't rule them out. As in the searches before, no leads from the Internet, so she began to follow her checklist; first the hospitals and then the morgues. *I'm sure that there are more ways to search, but I can't think of how.*

Two more months passed and she still found herself down a dead-end, dark alley with the building walls caving in. One-by-one the buildings would fall and crumble around her. At this point she prayed for just one piece of information, instead of having the walls disintegrate around her. She found it tiring to sneak around so they wouldn't find out and demand the search be stopped.

Spring was fast approaching and still it was getting harder and harder to find time to search. David's practice continued to grow, so she was also working more hours. Madison was becoming involved in more extracurricular activities that included voice and art lessons, and soccer practice, not to mention games every Saturday. Next week rehearsals for the school play started. It was almost too much to keep up with Madison and work, and still squeeze in time to privately search for her mom. She needed help, but discussing that with David was out of the question.

One more cup of coffee and then I'll be ready to drive to my old neighborhood, and if I still have the nerve, I'll stop the car and ask people what they remember.

Ellery wanted to personally talk with the couple who bought her childhood home. She chastised herself for being too scared to talk to neighbors before now.

She needed answers; hope to hold on to.

As she drove to the old neighborhood, memories replayed in her head. She remembered playing with the neighborhood kids every day in the summer and walking to school with them. She thought about Sam, who fell out of the tree and broke his arm, and about Halloween, running from house to house and getting as much candy as she could. Birthday parties, barbeques, ball games, and school events; and then, one-by-one, the weddings and moving away. She too had been one of the kids that married and moved away. Most of the parents had moved away, also.

Approaching her old street, Ellery slowed the car before pulling over. *What am I doing?* She swallowed hard and asked God to give her strength and courage to see this through. She continued down the street and saw the neighbor that lived on the north side of her old house. She waved, pulled into the yard, and with stomach churning, got out of the car.

"Hello, may I help you?" Maribeth asked.

"I hope so." Ellery pointed to her childhood home. "I grew up in that house and I haven't been back for a while. I'm Ellery Weber, formally Ellery Morgan. My mom is, Eleanor Morgan, and she recently moved without leaving a forwarding address. I am desperately trying to find her. Did she say anything to you?"

Did I just hear her right? She didn't know her mom moved? With a puzzled look she answered. "No. I was surprised to see a family move in. I was driving home the day the moving truck pulled out, but I didn't see your mom anywhere. A few days later, a new family moved in. It was the weirdest thing." Maribeth's mind was trying to figure out this lady and why she didn't know where her mom was.

"Thank you. Do you remember the name of the moving van?" Ellery was hoping the company would have a record of the trucks final destination.

"No, I really didn't take note. It took me a few seconds to realize that it was a moving van. I'm sorry." Maribeth answered.

Ellery pressed on. "Did any of the other neighbors say anything about all of this?"

Maribeth thought for a minute. "Yes. Helen, across the street, saw your mom get into a taxi with several pieces of luggage."

"This is more information than I have been able to find out in several months. Do you know what day the family moved in?" Ellery tried not to sound too eager.

"I can't remember, exactly." Maribeth said. "I know it was before Thanksgiving."

"Is Helen home? I would love to talk to her and see if she can provide me with more information." Ellery was impatient to talk to Helen and she sensed Maribeth didn't have any more information to give.

"Yes. Hey, just leave your car here."

"Thank you so much. For the first time, I have hope."

Maribeth couldn't help being curious as she watched Ellery make her way to Helen's door. *How does a mother leave and the daughter doesn't know? I'll talk to Helen later and see if Ellery gave her any more information. It is a mystery as to why it took so long for a daughter to come looking for her mom.*

Ellery walked across the street and rang the doorbell. As she stood there, she hoped all of this wouldn't turn out to be another dead end. It only took a few moments for Helen to open the door.

"Hello." Helen said.

"Hello. My name is Ellery Weber and my mom is Eleanor Morgan. Maribeth said you saw her leave in a taxi. Do you know what day that was and maybe the name on the taxi?" Ellery inquired.

"Well, let me see. It was quite a while back. I'm almost positive that it was several days before Thanksgiving. I don't think it was a cab, but maybe, an Uber instead." Helen looked confused. "Didn't your mother tell you she was leaving?"

Ellery's heart sank and tears threatened. She wasn't sure how to explain it or even if she should, but the older woman had eyes of immense compassion. "No. You see… we had a disagreement and I didn't speak to her for some time. I was ready to talk with her, but my husband wasn't and wouldn't let me see her. She was gone for more than a month before I knew it. My husband has finally softened enough to at least let me search for her."

"I see." Helen could see the pain in Ellery's eyes. "I'm so sorry you haven't been able to find your mom. She was the sweetheart of the neighborhood, even though I didn't know her very well. I heard about your dad. I'm sorry. He too was well thought of by all of us." Helen hoped this would give some comfort to Ellery.

"You are so kind. Thank you. This has been really hard on me and I don't even know why I shared as much as I did with you. If you think of anything else, please call me." Ellery said writing down her number.

Helen's heart went out to this young woman. "I can tell you want to keep this between the two of us, so I will be very discreet when I call."

"Thank you." Ellery left feeling more hopeful than she had in days. She knew it was only a small clue, but it gave her something new to cling to.

I'm out of time, I'll have to come back another day and talk to the people who bought Mom's house. I have just enough time to pick up Madison without being late. I'll check my calendar when I get home and see when I can find time to get away. I hope it's soon, so I don't lose my nerve in talking with other neighbors.

Madison was coming out of the door as Ellery pulled into the pick-up line. She seemed so happy; talking and laughing with her friends. Play tryouts were over and the list of who got what part would be posted tomorrow. Madison had tried out for one of the leads, but said she would be happy getting any part as long as she could be in the play.

"Hi, mom." Madison was beaming, as she waved goodbye to her friends.

"Hi, honey. Good day at school? How were tryouts?" Ellery asked, trying to sound upbeat.

"School was good. I got an A on my science test and an A- on my English paper. Tryouts were so much fun. I love all the parts, but I really want a leading role. They have more lines and you get to be on stage a lot." Madison said all in one breath. "What's for dinner tonight? I'm starved."

Ellery laughed at her daughter. "Well, we can either have leftovers or I can order pizza. Dad should be home when we get there and we'll see what he wants."

"Dad will want pizza over leftovers. I guarantee it." Madison replied.

Just as Ellery predicted, David was home when they got there. The verdict was in and all three wanted pizza. David said he would place the order and splurge by having it delivered.

Ellery was happy and wished she could share what she

found out today, but she didn't want anything to spoil her hope in finding her mother. It was a rare occasion that she could honestly say, all three in the house were happy and content.

Chapter 10
Living Life

Between teaching and selling her art work, Eleanor saved enough money to take a well-deserved vacation. She and Logan had always wanted to take an Alaskan cruise. The travel agent helped her plan a thirty-five-day trip, which included, not only an Alaskan cruise but land package to Denali, and then a separate excursion over the Canadian Rockies by rail. Eleanor soaked in all the information about what and how to pack, excursions to go on, and the best stateroom to book.

It was late July when Eleanor set out on her journey. She arrived at the St. Croix airport ready to experience everything she possibly could. It was a long flight, with three connecting flights, just to get to the start of her journey.

She arrived in Vancouver and boarded a van full of other excited travelers. Everyone was talking about starting their adventure through Alaska. The ship didn't set sail until tomorrow, so it was on to the hotel and then out to explore the sites of the city.

Hoping for a more personal experience on her trip, Eleanor reserved a balcony stateroom on a smaller cruise line. The room was not very large, but it was more than comfortable. The best part of the room was the balcony where she could enjoy the scenery while having a cup of coffee. It would also provide refuge when she needed to be alone with her thoughts and emotions.

Prince Rupert was the first stop. Eleanor thoughtfully selected each excursion, wanting to experience something new and different, something she may never have the chance to do again. For her first excursion she chose a sea plane which would travel to remote destinations. Hoping for amazing aerial views of the landscape and wildlife, she climbed aboard armed with camera and a creative eye.

The second full day was spent traveling through the inside passage. The weather was absolutely beautiful. For Eleanor it was as if an artist was he painting soft, bright blue brush strokes for the sky, passengers with hair blowing ever so slightly, and only a trace of white caps, giving a sense of peace and calm, as the ship glided through the waters.

"It's beautiful. Isn't it?" A lady next to her said.

"Words cannot describe it." Eleanor replied.

"Hi, I'm Terri. Terri Brooks. I've been waiting years to take this cruise and now that I'm here, it is more than I had hoped for. This day makes me wish the voyage would be forever."

Eleanor, sensing the woman wanted someone to talk with, continued the conversation. "Where are you from?"

"New York," she said. "I worked in retail for thirty years. I can't believe I'm willing to stand here after all the years of being on my feet. I loved my job, but my health and age started getting the best of me, so I retired."

"I trust it isn't a serious health issue." Eleanor said.

"Not serious, just annoying and achy at times. Arthritis in my knees, ankles, and hands. At times, it makes walking and doing certain things a challenge. So far, it hasn't been too bad on the trip."

"I know we have just met, but if you need someone to help you, especially on any of the excursions, I'm your girl." Eleanor suggested they take the chairs that had become available and enjoy the view in a more relaxing manner. Terri smiled and agreed. Her legs were getting tired and beginning to ache, but she didn't want to leave just yet.

The next several days the ship continued through the inside passage and the Misty Fjords, where she saw incredible views of glaciers, snowcapped peaks, majestic waterfalls, and brilliant, icy, blue lakes that glistened in the sun. *This must be where the idea of glitter came from. No matter where I point the camera, I'm getting postcard pictures.*

She and Terri met several times on deck and had a few meals together. Eleanor enjoyed her company and hearing all about living and working in New York City. She learned that Terri had never married. Her mother had passed away when Terri was in her twenties, so she moved in with her father to keep him company and take care of the house. He died several years ago, and Terri has been alone ever since.

Her friends either moved away or moved on, while she took care of her father. Her brothers and older sister all live in other states and once her father passed away, stopped making the trip to New York. "They call and text, but I miss seeing them. I miss the physical and personal connection. My nieces and nephews are all growing up and very few of them really remember me. I've had a good life, no regrets there, but I do regret being separated from my family. I miss them terribly. I also miss the friends that were once a constant in my life."

Eleanor felt a sort of kinship with Terri. Her situation is different, but in many ways the same. She, too is without family, but she has friends. She prayed that Terri would be able to meet new people and begin to get out more in New York. Eleanor suggested that she join some groups or community classes that interest her in order to meet people.

All of her excursions were wonderful, but she wished Logan was next to her. He would have found so much excitement and enjoyment seeing brown bears searching for fish or the eagles soaring high above the coastline. He would have been in awe whale watching in a vessel with large windows on the lower level that made you feel as though you were eye-to-eye with all the Alaskan sea life.

It was nearing the end of the cruise, and Eleanor was preparing to head further north on a smaller ship and then by train to Denali.

Not wanting to waste any time in Denali, Eleanor strapped on a helmet with a Go-Pro camera and joined a small group for ziplining. She walked with her fellow adventurers over a bridge to a platform high above the ground. A space which seemed far too small to hold all of them. Heart racing and palms sweaty, she took a nervous leap and was quickly racing through open air. She hoped no one had heard her cry of fear.

Gliding through the trees with the wind hitting her face, she was weightless and free while soaring high above the ground. Below her was an array of lush foliage, animals, and the rushing water from a nearby waterfall. Laughing, she wondered if the wildlife thought she looked as strange as she felt. The first landing platform aggressively jarred her entire body, like someone had suddenly pulled the emergency stop cord on a train. Without hesitation and only a thin wire to hold her, she leaped off the second platform. She was once again gliding freely through the air, seeing massive mountains in the distance dressed in all shades of green.

Finishing the zip line she rushed to join the last guided horseback trip along the trails. The ride was quiet and gentle, through the same area she had just soared over. What a difference between looking down over the vast area and riding through looking up, only seeing a focused snapshot of what was immediately around you.

Trying to get out of bed that next morning was met with some difficulty. The previous day proved to be a bit too much for Eleanor. Moaning and groaning, she made it to the shower. She stayed in it longer than usual letting the hot water pour over her aching body. By the time she went down for breakfast, her body was moving at a more normal pace and without as many winces of pain, although the remnants of the previous day were still very much with her.

She saw Mike and Samantha Owens struggling to walk without grimacing in pain and caught their eyes. "I take it both of you had too much excitement yesterday, also?"

Mike laughed loudly. "Yes, the zip line and horseback

riding should have been done about twenty years ago. It was so much fun we kept going, thinking we were thirty again. Now look at us, paying for it with every aching muscle."

"I understand," Eleanor said. "I was hoping for either a hot tub or a spa, but there is no time. I hope the riverboat is gentle."

"So, do I," Samantha said.

It was time to say farewell to Denali and all its splendor and board the riverboat for travel on the Chena River to Fairbanks. This would end her Alaskan journey. Eleanor was thankful for a comfortable bed that night before starting the third leg of her adventure – a twelve-day trip through the Canadian Rockies.

She boarded the train and saw that all the seats allowed for perfect views of mountains and icy waterfalls. train followed the Sea to Sky Highway as it traveled towards Whistler. Eleanor had plenty of time to explore. After participating in a few calm and scenic excursions, Eleanor made her way to a more adventurous activity – jet boating.

"I will only be here once, so why not try it. It may jolt my entire body, but it's worth it. That is, if I don't fall out." She said to a young couple in the group.

The young couple laughed and said they would grab on to her if she started to go over. They had been on jet boats several times and loved it. Laughing, they boarded the boat.

She was much older than the other passengers and was now questioning her wisdom for such a ride.

She found her adrenaline pumping as she jetted at a high rate of speed, bouncing across great pools of water. The ride was an exhilarating rollercoaster with added aspects of cold and wet. Even though fast, she was able to take in the cloudless blue sky, spot bald eagles, moose, bear fishing for food, and other wildlife along the river banks.

Feet back on shore, she grabbed a quick lunch and a much needed hot cup of coffee. After lunch, Eleanor took a quiet walk to Whistler Lake. She spent time sketching, reading, and just enjoying the splendor of God's handiwork. Thinking about Logan and how much she missed him was still a constant pain in her heart. *All this trip has to offer and no one to share it with.* She was content, but still alone.

She was half way back to the hotel when she heard an unfamiliar sound. Pausing, Eleanor looked around. After a quick glance she found she was the only person on the trail. The sound, she saw came from a large bear standing in the road about fifty yards ahead of her. The hotel was in sight, but the bear stood between she and safety. *The guide told us about bears and what to do if you encounter one, but my mind, at the moment, is blank.*

Time was frozen and so was Eleanor. The bear suddenly took note of Eleanor and gave a frightening growl. She translated the growl as, "run and I'll hunt you down or stay and you are definitely mine." Eleanor began to remember what they said to do. She slowly took out her bear spray as she made her body as large as she could. Hands in the air while yelling at the bear. She prayed this would work. *I go on a trip of a lifetime only to be eaten by a bear.*

The bear started to make a move towards her. Her body told her to run, but she forced her mind to take control. She again, raised her arms, this time putting her backpack in the air. When the bear stopped, she slowly walked backwards on very rubbery legs with the bear spray at the ready. Once again, the bear started moving towards her. She was sure the bear could hear her heart beating and smell the sweat dripping out of every pore in her body. Eleanor was preparing to be eaten. It was like a chess game. Precise, calculated moves until one would say checkmate, or in this case, check-meat.

Just then she heard a group of people behind her. She hoped they would scare the bear off instead of causing it to make a quick attack. The guide in the group saw the bear, stopped, and began to yell loudly while waving his arms. The rest of the group followed his lead. The bear stopped and for the next few minutes looked at Eleanor and then the others. Giving a last snort, it slowly walked off the path and back into the woods.

Everyone continued to stand still until the guide signaled it was safe to move. "Lady, are you okay?"

Eleanor could only nod that she was alright. Her body was jello and her mind mush. She gratefully allowed two of the men to be the solid support she needed. The group walked slowly back to the hotel, mostly in silence, but a few replaying what had happened only moments before. Eleanor retreated to her room after being check out by the hotel doctor. She wanted the trembling to stop. It was a night for room service, reflection, and thanking God for keeping her safe.

Eleanor was in awe as she looked up in the sky and watched the Aurora Borealis. "It's truly magnificent. I thought we had seen all of God's awesome wonders, until now." Her camera rapidly capturing the event.

"It is." Miriam replied. "It's truly amazing."

"I wonder if anything can top this?" John said.

Eleanor put her camera down and enjoyed the miracles of God's creation and the peaceful night. She wished there was some way to capture this in real time and share it with the world. She wished, once again, she could share it with Logan. Her heart felt empty tonight even with the millions of stars above.

The next day Eleanor arrived at Lake Louise. She did something she hadn't done in years; a spa treatment. She decided to take advantage of the full spa and salon services by scheduling a massage, relaxation facial, manicure, and pedicure. When it was all done she found herself so relaxed, she slept for two hours. Awake and hungry, and wanting time to relax, reflect, and plan her few remaining days, she ordered room service. Like her daughter, she was a planner.

The time spent sitting at Lake Louise was most relaxing for her, with its vibrant turquoise hues, and iridescent colors from the different lights and angles, giving off a brilliant sheen. The late summer colors, with the glaciers and lakes, were the perfect background to reflect on the last several days. She did some quick sketches during the trip, but today she was relaxed and focused on detail as she drew. Some of the sketches she would possibly frame and others, she would paint. Even though, somewhat alone at the lake, Eleanor felt less alone than she had in the last few years. God was beginning to heal her heart.

Eleanor made a last minute decision to whitewater raft down the Kicking Horse River. The water was going to be cold, so hopefully, the heavy rain gear would keep her fairly dry and warm. The company offered a scenic ride or a wild ride. Scenic was perfect for Eleanor, but the group voted for the wild ride; and wild it was. She strapped the Go Pro camera to the helmet and with shaky legs got in the raft. She believed that if she survived a bear, she could survive this.

The well-experienced guide was constantly yelling out which way to lean or how to paddle. The water was icy cold and the thought of falling in brought hypothermia to mind. At each bend she held her breath not knowing what would happen next as waves threatened to swallow them. The raft passed jagged rocks and giant boulders where she envisioned her body being put through a paper shredder.

It was hard to make anything out as everything went by fast and even life itself became a blur. An eternity went by according to Eleanor, even though the guide said it was a short trip. Shocked, she made it to land, alive and in one piece. She climbed out of the raft with every muscle in her body beginning a rebellion. Each step gave the rebellion a new victory.

On the final night before heading back to Vancouver, sleep escaped her, like the fly you can never get rid of. She spent the night tossing and turning. Her mind wouldn't shut down as she replayed every day of her trip.

Once on the train, the conductor stored her carry-on. Before settling in for the ten-hour trip to Vancouver, she asked the conductor for a pillow and blanket. She chuckled as she watched the other passengers take their seats, having the same thought as she, asking for pillows and blankets. Not very long after the train pulled out of the station, Eleanor found her eyelids closing at the same time her mind was giving in to a deep sleep. A few hours later, she woke up hungry and thirsty.

After lunch, Eleanor took out her book to do a little reading, but instead, fell into another deep sleep. It was already 3:30 p.m. and the train was due in Vancouver around 6 p.m. She had slept most of the time, and looking around most of the other passengers had followed suit. She picked up her book and found this time she could read and not fall asleep.

A loud clashing of metal pierced her ears. Eleanor and others were violently thrust into the air. Luggage, food, and clothing were mixed in with the bodies as they fought to land. She came down with the same intensity of being ejected from her seat, however, she landed on something soft. Several pieces of luggage were on top of her and she realized that her soft landing was because of a body she fell on.

Somehow, Eleanor managed to move her body off of the unmoving person underneath her. She felt for a pulse. It was there, faint, but he was alive. Chaos was in the air. She heard screams of fear. Screams of pain. Screams for help. The air was thick with dust. She couldn't see an exit. She couldn't see anyone; she could only hear the screams. She was in pain, but getting out of the train was more important. She had to find an exit, then she would come back and try to get the man out. The dust thinned enough for her to see the exit about twenty-five yards ahead. She began to crawl, moaning in pain with each move.

Finally reaching the exit, she found that it was above her. The train car was on its side. Thankfully a few others had made it to the same exit and were assisting each other in getting out. Eleanor mentioned the man that was still alive, but she couldn't drag him out.

"We'll go get him after we get all of you out. The train isn't on fire, just a lot of dust. Are your arms badly hurt or can you lift yourself up to the opening?" A man said.

"My entire body is in pain, but I don't think anything is broken. I think I can make it, especially with some help." Eleanor told the man.

Eleanor softly cried out in pain as they lifted her out up and out of the train. Once outside, she saw devastation. People were bleeding, some with mangled limbs. There was crying and moaning. Some were looking for loved ones and friends. She made her way to a small group of people who were bleeding. She ripped up a shirt and made bandages. She moved on to others, telling them that help was on the way.

So far, to Eleanor, it looked like everyone had survived, until she saw a body not moving. It was the conductor. She prayed he was alive, but her stomach lurched as she approached. The sweet, gentle man was dead.

It took an hour before all the emergency crews arrived. Eleanor climbed into a van with others not seriously injured to be transported to a hospital thirty miles away. The more seriously hurt were put into waiting ambulances. It was a horrific day, but Eleanor survived. She sent her prays of thanks upward and her pleas for others to be okay. At the end of the day, five were dead and eight in critical condition, including the man who softened her landing, probably saving her from serious injury.

Tomorrow, she would leave Vancouver and begin the long journey home. Home sounded good.

Chapter 11
Life and Death

Madison was having a great summer. She continued art and voice lessons, helped paint set designs at the community play house, and most recently, spent a week at summer camp. She enjoyed the time at home with her parents and going to the beach on weekends. In two weeks, they were all going to Disneyland. She had never been there and was counting down the days until it was time to leave.

Ellery was worried that Madison was pushing herself too hard this summer. For the past two days, she hadn't had much of an appetite and was tired most of the time. Today she complained that her neck and head hurt. Ellery gave her something for the pain and told her to lie down for a while. She checked on her and found her sleeping, but restless.

She was glad David came home early and wasted no time in voicing her concern. "Madison has been tired for the last two days and hasn't had much of an appetite. I'm a little worried."

"She's probably feeling the delayed effect of camp life. I'm sure she'll bounce back in a few more days." David said hoping to put Ellery at ease.

"Well, today she's had a severe headache and said her neck hurt. I gave her something for the pain and sent her to bed. She's been sleeping for the last four hours." Ellery saw David's expression changed.

Uneasiness settled over him with what Ellery had just said. "Really? This doesn't sound like a girl whose been too busy and is just run down. Maybe she's coming down with something. Let's go up and check on her."

Together they went to Madison's room. Opening the door slowly, in case she was sleeping, they both looked in. Panic shot through them as they saw Madison on the floor. David rushed to his daughter and found her burning with fever.

"Madison. Madison!" David called out to her.

Ellery felt like she was in a dream. She took the cell phone out of her pocket and called the doctor. After giving him the symptoms for the last few days, he told her to call an ambulance immediately. He would be there soon.

David heard Ellery's voice quiver as she spoke with the doctor and gathered that he too must be concerned. The fear in her eyes said even more.

The ambulance arrived within minutes. He and Ellery stood helpless as paramedics took her vitals and conveyed them to the hospital. Madison still hadn't shown any signs of waking up.

"David, she's so hot and lifeless. What do you think it is?" David had a suspicion, but for now, kept it to himself. He didn't need Ellery to be any more upset than she already was. Before he could form a response, they were told Madison was ready to transport.

"Ellery, you ride in the ambulance with her and I'll meet you at the hospital." David took her arm and walked her to the door of the ambulance.

"Are you sure?" Ellery asked.

"Yes. If she wakes up, she needs to know one of us is there. I'm not sure you are in any condition to drive. I don't think I'm much better, but I'll be right behind the ambulance."

"I need you to go in with us. Will you park and hurry to go in with us?" Ellery asked, trying to hold it together.

"I will get in with you. If you don't see me, I'll find Doctor Davis and have him get me back to the room." David assured her.

Ellery got in the ambulance and David quickly followed as close as he could. Every time she looked back, her daughter looked the same; lifeless. The hospital wasn't that far, but it seemed to be taking an eternity to get there. She couldn't see out the back and prayed David was close behind.

Arriving at the hospital emergency entrance, Ellery jumped out and looked quickly for David before hurrying to the back of the ambulance. She saw David running towards her and breathed a sigh of relief. He would be with her.

"I grabbed the first parking spot I found and started running." David was breathing heavily. "I think I'm a bit out of shape."

They quickly followed behind the paramedics through the emergency entrance. Doctor Davis was there along with several other doctors and nurses. They started to follow the gurney into the room, but were stopped.

"David. Ellery. We need you to stay out here while we examine Madison. I promise to come out immediately when I know something." Doctor Davis said with compassion.

They sat in chairs outside the room. Doctors and nurses were going in and out of the room. Equipment and vials of blood went in and out. David put his arm around Ellery and prayed for his daughter, and then for the doctors. He wanted to know if his suspicions were correct before calling his pastor. He decided it was time to let Ellery know what he suspected.

"Ellery. Some of Madison's symptoms are … well, I think … Madison may have Meningitis."

Ellery put her hand to her mouth while her eyes pleaded with David to tell her why he thinks that.

"I'm not sure, but the symptoms match what I know about the disease. I pray I'm wrong. If it is, she may have a long recovery ahead of her," he said.

An hour went by before Doctor Davis came out to talk to them. "We ran many tests and they all came back with the same results. Madison has bacterial meningitis."

Ellery grabbed David's hand, as the color drained from her face. "Will she recover? When can we see her?"

David held her hand tightly, as he waited for the doctor to give them more information.

"Madison is very sick. We are starting her on penicillin to treat the infection and also corticosteroids to reduce the swelling in her brain. We will be moving her to intensive care so she can be closely monitored. You can go in and see her for a few minutes. Once they have her in a room, you will be allowed to go in and sit with her."

"Thank you doctor. Are we allowed to spend the night or is there somewhere close by we can stay?" David asked. "We don't want to be far in case she, or you, need us."

"Unfortunately, no. However, you can stay in the lounge just down the hall. You will be notified of any changes and most definitely when she regains consciousness. The lounge has several recliners. I'll have the staff bring you pillows and blankets."

"David. Ellery. The next several days are critical. You may be asked to leave the room at times and your cooperation is important to the work a doctor or nurse must do."

Ellery swallowed hard, but she had to know. "What are her chances?"

"Right now, fifty percent. Each day she responds to the antibiotics, her chances increase. I wish I had better news. One more very important question. Has she been around other people, especially kids, in the last week?"

"Yes." Ellery said. "She came home from camp two days ago. She's been tired and not eating, but we thought she was just rundown."

"This is a contagious disease. Can you please write down the name of the camp and any contact information? We need to notify them immediately."

"Could Madison have gotten it there? What about the other kids? Are you saying she could have infected them?" Ellery went to stand, but her knees grew weak. David put his arm around her and held her close.

"Those are the unknown questions at this time. It could be someone at camp was a carrier and other kids may have been infected also. We need to let people know so we can track this and make sure it doesn't spread. It doesn't mean Madison is the cause. One more thing. I need you both to step into this room and a nurse will draw blood. We must make sure you are not infected."

"Thank you again, doc. Let's go see Madison and then head to ICU to wait. Can we fill out the information in ICU?"

"That's fine. Give the forms to the nurse at the desk when you're done. You will need to wear protective gowns and masks when in the room with Madison. I'll be back in the morning to check on her. The hospital will call me if there is any change."

Pastor Stithers arrived late that night and sat with them. Together they prayed for Madison's recovery and strength for David and Ellery. He left an hour later with the promise he would be back tomorrow.

David called the dentists at his office and the office manager, Marge, to inform them what was happening and that he wouldn't be in for the rest of the week. He asked if they would cover as many patients as possible and then reschedule the rest. He would try and find someone that could fill in for the rest of this week and possibly next. They all wished Madison the best and told him not to worry.

David then called his sister and other relatives to let them know. All of them were concerned and some offered to fly in to help, if needed. David wasn't sure what they needed at this time.

"I wish one of my relatives was a dentist." He said to Ellery.

"What about calling the university? Maybe they have a student ready to graduate, or even a graduate that could fill in temporarily. It would give them some experience and they would be under the guidance of the staff." Ellery suggested.

"That's an excellent idea! I'll call the office tomorrow and ask Marge to check it out." David smiled at Ellery, "This is going to be a rough road for all of us, but I'm confident Madison will pull through."

Madison was in and out of consciousness for several days and remained in intensive care for two weeks. She was finally moved to the unit just outside of the ICU, where they would continue to monitor her. Madison was still very weak and the doctors all agreed she needed months of therapy to get back the full function of her muscles. She had now been given an 80/20 chance for a full recovery. Her fight continued.

A month in the hospital gave Madison time to think about herself, her parents, her future, and her gramma. She began to regret what she had done and started slipping into depression. The doctors worried if she didn't pull out of it, her recovery may be twice as long, or not at all.

Madison had stared at the Bible next to her bed for days. She slowly picked it up and began to read. She started looking for verses about lying and hate. As she read them, her mind and heart began to question her past actions. Several verses laid heavy on her young heart. She read how the Lord hates liars. *God must detest me. Will He ever love me again?* She read that God tells us to keep our mouth from telling lies. *I told really bad lies that were evil.*

A few days later she read lying and spreading lies makes a person a fool. *I am a fool. I let jealousy and hate destroy my family. I can't even tell Grampa I'm sorry.* One verse kept playing over and over in her mind. Philippians 2:3, "Do nothing out of selfish ambition or vain conceit. Rather, in humility value others above yourselves." She realized clearly, for the first time, that she had put herself first. She never thought about her mom or gramma.

Madison started to talk to God for the first time in years. Oh, she prayed, but never really talked to God. She never really wanted God to control her life. But now, her heart was broken and open to what God was telling her. *I just thought I could get my own way and everyone would be happy. How am I going to make this right? How will Mom and Dad ever forgive me? Why did I hurt Gramma this way?* She prayed harder than she had in her whole life for the next hour. She had listened to her chat group members instead of God.

"Good morning, sweetheart. How are you doing today? Breakfast any good, or would you like this Egg McMuffin and Strawberry Smoothie from McDonalds?"

This put a smile on Madison's face. "Tough choice, but I'll take McDonalds. You can feel free to have my hospital breakfast."

"Thanks, but I'll pass." Ellery laughed. "I see you have therapy in an hour. Is it going any better?"

"No. I wish I could just be back to me. Walking and running. I miss my friends." Madison said. "I know. I know. Patience. Who came up with that word anyway?"

"I've often wondered that myself. I'm not going to tell you that you'll only be in therapy for a few days and then get back to normal. But, you have always been persistent to get what you want, no matter how long it takes. This is just another challenge for you."

"I know, but it's harder than anything else I've had to do."

"You could set goals and mark your progress each week or day. We could figure out a reward system for you, like, an ice cream sundae, or a new art tablet."

"I suppose." Madison answered.

"Hey, I just thought of something." Ellery noticing her

daughter was somewhat apathetic. "You are well enough for your art supplies. Any chance you would want them?"

"Sure, if it's not too much trouble."

Her response was somewhat uninterested, but Ellery smiled and told her she'd bring them the next time she came.

"Are you and Dad coming tonight?" Madison asked.

"Yes. Do you want us to bring dinner, or is there a hospital special tonight?"

"Funny, Mom. You could bring pizza."

"Done. You have therapy in about five minutes, and I have to get going. Dad and I will be back with the pizza. I love you." Ellery kissed her daughter goodbye.

"Love you too, Mom."

Madison let her mom's words sink in, "You have been persistent to get what you want, no matter how long it takes." *I was persistent with Gramma and got what I thought I wanted.*

David and Ellery returned with pizza, as promised. Ellery noticed her daughter was very quiet all through dinner and assumed it was because she was tired. David seemed to notice also and tried to strike up conversations that she would engage in. Madison did her best, but she had something on her mind. Something she had to tell her parents. It was going to be the hardest thing for her to do, but she had to do it. She tried to find reasons to keep the truth to herself, but she couldn't ignore the voice inside. She couldn't go on anymore with this burden – with this guilt.

Madison pushed her plate to the side and looked at her parents. "Mom. Dad. I need to tell you something. After I tell you, you may hate me. I'm prepared for you to be angry, yell, and maybe never forgive me. You may not even want to see me for a few days."

"Madison. We love you and nothing you have done, said, or will do, will ever change that." David said. "Now what do you have to tell us?"

Tears started to roll down her cheeks before deep, uncontrollable sobs ravaged her body. David and Ellery held their daughter and tried to calm her. After several minutes, Madison was able to bring herself under control and begin to tell them what had her so upset.

"I … was … jealous …" Madison stammered. She took a deep breath and then slowly poured out everything in her heart. "I was so jealous of Gramma and Grampa, but more of Gramma. I thought if she was out of the way, even for a few weeks, I could have you all to myself. I was tired of sharing holidays and Sundays with them. When they were around, I wasn't the center of your attention. I began to believe they were more important. But, I never thought of the consequences. I didn't know Grampa was going to die. I didn't know Gramma wouldn't fight back and instead move away. I never thought about how hurt Mom would be and how much tension it would cause. It was great for a while, but then, I regretted what I had done, but couldn't bring myself to tell you. I convinced myself that I didn't do anything wrong."

Ellery went to speak, but Madison held up her hand. "I made up everything about Gramma. It started when you went to that conference. I yelled at her and told her I hated her."

Fighting back tears and the urge to scream, Ellery could not believe what she was hearing. David's eyes went from Madison to Ellery. He had kept his wife from her mother because he believed his daughter. He wouldn't even let Eleanor explain her side or try to work things out. Madison wasn't the only one who caused Eleanor to leave. He played a part, also. Anger began to over-take him.

Madison continued. "Every time Gramma was near me, I would whisper 'I hate you' or say, 'I wish you were dead'. When Grampa died, I told her that I wished it had been her. She never lost her temper and after the first few times, never showed any emotion. I think Grampa knew, but he never said anything either. I knew I had the upper hand when I realized Gramma wasn't going to tell you what I was doing."

David's anger could no longer be controlled and he exploded. "How could you do this? How could you purposefully hurt so many? I believed you. You made me part of your scheme!" David's cheeks were hot coals and his lips curled with disgust. He walked to the window and stared out trying to hold back the maddening screams that wanted to be release at his daughter.

Madison started to respond, but she was interrupted by Ellery.

"I agree with your dad! How could you? I've ached for my mom every day and couldn't tell anyone. I don't know if she is sick or even alive. She has no one!" Ellery continued to look at her daughter. Digging her nails into her crossed arms, she hated what her daughter did and at the same time felt guilty for her feelings.

Madison could hardly see through the liquid that filled her eyes. *I hurt my parents and now they are pulling away from me. Will they abandon me like I made them do with Gramma?*

David turned back to Madison, still seething and ready to release another barrage of accusations, until he saw the look on her face. His anger was suddenly brought under control, to some degree. He needed to help his daughter but his emotions were raw. A storm raged inside knowing he should deal with his guilt and sin later, but wanting to do it now. "Madison, I am shocked and disappointed in you.

"David." Ellery touched his arm to signal, not to say anything else.

"No. I have to. It's important." David said. "I let my emotions sway me. Madison, I let hate fill my heart so much that I wouldn't give your gramma a chance to defend herself. I cut her off from everyone. I convinced Mom you were being abused by an evil woman. I denied her to speak or even search for Gramma. So yes, I am mad at what you did; but more for the part I've played."

Madison found it difficult to look at her parents. Her eyes went everywhere except to them. "I don't know if you'll ever forgive me, but I want to find Gramma. I need her to know what I did. I want Mom's heart to stop hurting."

Ellery looked at her daughter. "I'm hurt and I'm angry. It's hard to even process all of this. It's hard not to scream. It's even hard to breathe. Part of me wants to walk out the door and yet part of me wants to cry and tell you everything will be alright. When did you plan all of this?"

Madison explained to her parents about the chat room. She detailed the conversations and how they encouraged and persuaded her that it was something she had to do. "They convinced me that it would get worse and I would soon be ignored and left out."

"Madison." David said. "I can't stay here and pretend not be angry. I think it best that Mom and I leave before we say something we'll regret later. I feel like I'm on the scrambler ride at the fair, everything moving fast and crisscrossing in all directions. We will be back tomorrow to talk about this more. Maybe I won't feel so outraged and betrayed come morning. I won't promise though." David knew he had to get out of that room and fast. He told Ellery he would wait in the hall for her.

Ellery stood there for a few minutes weighing her words. Approaching Madison slowly, she said, "It was hard for you to tell us, I'm sure. But, you have dealt us an unforeseeable shock. And it's not easy to respond right now. Your dad has been betrayed by your lies and I have lost my mother. Your dad and I still love you, but right now, we are hurt beyond words." Ellery bent down and kissed her daughter's forehead. I'll see you tomorrow. Try and rest.

Madison buried her head in the pillow and wept. She couldn't bear to watch her mom walk out of the room and possibly her life. *Is this what Gramma felt? Did her heart hurt this bad? I don't deserve to get well again. I don't deserve to walk or run again.*

Chapter 12
Post Confession

David and Ellery walked slowly and silently through the hospital. The silence continued on the ride home. Each looking at the other, wishing someone would say something. However, both were stubborn, angry, hurt, and harboring resentment and blame. Their mouths were cemented shut.

Ellery finally broke down, as they entered the living room. "I'm so furious! How could she do this and keep it a secret all these years? You. You encouraged her. You didn't even give my mom a chance. The last phone call she made was to say goodbye, and all she could do was leave a message – I love you."

David could only hang his head and remain silent. It took a few minutes before he responded. "I'm sorry, Ellery.

I got caught up in our daughter being hurt and I believed every word she said. I'm ashamed." Regret laid heavy on his heart and guilt ripped through every vein in his body.

Ellery's anger came to the surface. "I know you believed everything Madison told you. You and I believed it without question or evidence. We ignored all the signs. We refused to enter any other reason in our mind, other than what she told us. I got over my anger and distrust. I wanted to talk to Mom and hear what she had to say. But you, you would go into a rage if I mentioned it. It was like I didn't know you."

"I didn't know you missed your mom so much. I guess I never really took the time to notice or didn't want to notice. Sure, I saw how much you missed her during the holidays, but I miss my parents during holidays." David sat powerless to repair the damage.

Ellery continued to speak, not noticing David's slumped shoulders and trembling hands. "I know how convincing Madison could be. I too, was convinced at first, but I thought it would get resolved and we could be happy again. I believed my mom would be welcomed back into our home. You and Madison seemed happy not to have her in our lives. It didn't take the holidays before I missed Mom. I started missing her a few weeks after Dad's funeral.

David's voice became shaky. "I made it hard for you... for you to talk to me about your mom. I was angry and bitter whenever you brought it up. I gave in to hate because of what she had done to our daughter. I was seething to think someone close to us could hurt our Madison. I was unforgiving in that respect and I hardened my heart to ever believing she was innocent. I knew you had been searching for her, but you never shared anything, so I hoped you had given up…"

Ellery interrupted. She wanted to speak her mind. She had waited long enough. "You and Madison would become irritated, even explosive, if I mentioned her name. When Pastor Harris told us she had left, my heart sank and I fell apart internally. I had to carry all of this alone. Neither you nor Madison cared that she had disappeared. You actually seemed relieved that she was permanently gone."

"You have every right to be angry at Madison and even more so at me. I have caused you and your mother pain and on top of it all, I drove her away." He was choking trying to get his words out. "My mind was clouded with lies and I was blinded to the truth. I refused to listen to God. Please … forgive … me." Today his emotions flowed freely.

Ellery reached for David and together they wept.

The conversation continued, with Ellery speaking first. "I was almost to the point of seeking professional help for my depression. I didn't want to cause problems with you and Madison, so I tried to deal with everything myself. I began searching and even went to talk to a few of her old neighbors. I was waiting for a time to go back and speak with the people who bought my old home, but I got so busy and then Madison got sick."

"I'm so ashamed I let my heart and mind fill with anger. I don't know if you can ever forgive me, but I hope in time, you will." David's eyes were pleading.

"I'll get over my anger in time. I do forgive you." Ellery said, as she took his hand. "I want to move on. I feel guilty for walking out on Madison tonight. I had so much anger in me that I was afraid to say too much to her. I don't want to show it anymore in front of our daughter.

"We have much to talk and pray about. I agree we shouldn't show our anger in front of Madison, even though what she did was wrong. She will have to face the guilt and the consequences and so will I." David said.

I'm afraid that my being careful in front of Madison makes you the target of my emotions." Ellery was now sorry for her earlier outburst.

What I do know, is we need to start searching for your mom together."

"Thank you."

The next morning, Ellery entered Madison's room first. "Good morning, Madison. You don't look like you slept much last night. Dad and I didn't sleep either.

"Good morning pal." David said as he walked in the room. "We left last night upset and angry; and worried about you and our reaction. Madison, we want you to understand this will take time. I am still angry with what you did and also what I did, but we love you, no matter what."

Madison tried to smile, but the guilt still crushed her heart. "Thank you. I don't deserve you being so nice to me. I don't even deserve you coming to see me today after what I did. I went to the chat room and told them I've been sick. I also let them know that their advice was wrong and I hurt so many people. I left the chat room for good.

"I'm sorry you've carried this burden alone for so many years. We all had a part in Gramma leaving. Your dad and I didn't take time to think about your accusations or ask questions. It happened so quickly after Grampa died, that we simply jumped to our own conclusions. We were willing to believe anything. We have a lot to discuss." Ellery added.

David was quick to add, "I'm glad you quit the chat room. Mom said what we both had on our minds. It's time to move forward and deal with the actions and consequences of our behaviors."

Madison finally asked the question she had wrestled with all night. "What can we do to find Gramma? I want her back in my life. I want Mom's heart to stop aching. We don't know where she is."

Ellery reassured her daughter. "Instead of me searching, we can all search. She's out there somewhere and I know she misses us."

"Will Gramma ever forgive me? I don't see why she would. I've been a horrible granddaughter." The tears rolled down Madison' face.

"We will all ask for her forgiveness and, because she is one of the most Christ-like people I know, I am certain she will forgive us." David assured his daughter.

"Madison." Ellery painfully watched her daughter struggle with what she had done. She was certain the tears fell all night. "I'm so glad you told us. I miss my mom terribly and I've been searching for her as much as I've been able to. I didn't want to upset you or Dad, so I didn't get to search a lot."

"Can we continue to search? Please?" Madison asked.

"We will talk more, I promise, but you have therapy in a few minutes. What do you say? I want you well enough to come home in the next few weeks." David answered.

"Your father's right, honey." Ellery added. "We love you. We'll see you later. Hey, you want us to bring lunch?"

Madison crinkled her nose. "Duh."

During next few weeks, the tension of what Madison had done began to ease. Conversations became more relaxed and light-hearted. Madison was stronger and scheduled to go home in a few days. David had rearranged his schedule to allow him to be home on Friday afternoons. Ellery continued with her leave of absence from work, so she could be with Madison as much as possible.

The day they had all been waiting for arrived. Madison was coming home. Ellery spent hours cleaning the house, putting fresh flowers in her room, purchasing more art supplies, and baking Madison's favorite cookies. She was still weak, and had to walk with a cane, but the therapists predicted the cane was needed for only a few more weeks. They were amazed at how well she responded to therapy and that her attitude and determination were the reasons for her quick recovery.

Madison had missed more than a month of school and was worried about going back. She had kept up with her core studies as best she could, but was still behind. She knew it was time to talk to her parents about being homeschooled. She addressed her parents that night at dinner. "I'm worried that I'm way behind in school. I haven't even been able to study until a few weeks ago. I don't want to go back just yet."

They were silent for a moment before David spoke. "You have obviously had this on your mind for a while. We didn't know you were struggling with the decision about going back to school, so what are you thinking?"

"I know mom has been waiting to get back to work, but I would like to be homeschooled." Madison said.

"If your dad and the office could do without me, I would love to be your teacher. I think we could get you caught up by the semester break, and then we'll look at options after that. What do you think?" Ellery looked at David.

He saw the smile on Madison's face and the longing in Ellery's eyes. "Well, she is a valuable employee and my right hand at the office. But, I believe her most important job is to take care of you, Madison." There was a yell from Madison before David could finish.

Ellery got up to hug and kiss her husband. "I think I have the best family ever. Thank you!"

Madison was almost giddy as she hugged her parents. "I will be the best student. Okay, we have to get books or see if the school will let me continue using what they gave me. I only have the four subjects, but would love to add electives. I don't want to do summer school to make up for lost credits. Is this possible?"

"Slow down, Madison," Ellery laughed. "I will contact the area homeschool association and they will know what you need to meet the state requirements for graduation. We can go see them tomorrow. Is that soon enough?"

"Perfect." Madison said. May I be excused? I'm a little tired and I want to do some painting."

"Excused." Ellery and David said simultaneously.

The next day, Ellery checked with the public high school to inquire if homeschool credits would be accepted. Then, she and Madison went to the homeschool building to find out more about requirements and how credits worked. They were pleased with what they learned and went to the bookstore before leaving to purchase books and look at some elective options.

"Do you know if I can do anything for an elective?" Madison asked the lady behind the desk.

"Almost anything." She said. "You need to plan it out, make sure you do enough hours, and it should be something related to academics, the trades, or personal interest; such as art or music."

Ellery winked at her daughter, knowing what she was thinking. They finished finding the needed books and school supplies before heading home to start planning.

Madison started working on her studies, including private art classes twice a week. She began documenting everything regarding their search for Gramma. David proposed setting aside time on Sunday afternoons for the family to share notes and plan out next steps.

"Ellery." David said. "I think it's time that you and I talk to the owners of your mom's old house and maybe more of the neighbors. Someone must have seen or heard something.

The new owners should be able to tell us who the realtor was and when the house was sold."

"I agree. Even when I had some time to return, I was too scared to go back and ask questions. I didn't want to be disappointed. But, it's time. It will be much easier for me with you going along." Ellery said.

"Should I come or would it be better if I stayed here?" Madison asked.

Ellery knew her daughter wanted to be a part of this search. "This time, I think you should stay here. Three people asking questions may make them a little nervous."

"I don't like it, but I understand. Please, don't forget to give me all the details. Remember, I have to chart and document all of this for school." Madison said, a little disappointed.

David picked Ellery up after work and started for her childhood neighborhood. They were hoping to talk to people between getting home from work and dinner. David seemed optimistic, but Ellery held to her reserve.

They pulled up in front of her old home and got out of the car. As they approached the front door, a man came around the corner.

"May I help you?" He asked.

"I hope so. I'm David Weber and this is my wife, Ellery. She grew up in this house and her mom sold it a few years ago. We haven't been able to locate Eleanor Morgan since then. Do you and your wife have time to answer a few questions? It won't take long. We are trying to piece together the sale and maybe where she moved to."

"Yes, of course. I'm Jason Levine. Please come in."

Walking into the living room, Ellery took note that the new owners hadn't made many changes, other than paint and new flooring. Jason called to his wife while Ellery and David took a seat on the sofa.

"Caitlyn, this is David and Ellery Weber. They want to ask us some questions about the lady we bought the house from."

"Hello, it's nice to meet you. I'm a bit confused, but if I can help, I will." Caitlyn said.

David briefly explained the reason for the visit and then began to ask questions. They learned that Eleanor was very secretive during the entire process and that her realtor had handled everything. They never met her or her realtor. However, the realtor's name was on the closing paperwork. Caitlyn gave the paperwork to Ellery allowing her to write the information down, including the Levine's realtor.

Jason told them the closing and move in dates. "Your mom was already moved out at the time of closing. We never saw a moving truck. Sorry we can't be of more help. Hope this information will be of some use."

David and Ellery thanked the Levine's and left. It was too late to talk with anyone else in the neighborhood. Another trip needed to be scheduled to ask the other neighbors what they knew. They had just been given a small nugget of hope, but was it enough to find Eleanor? Ellery prayed it would be and that it wouldn't be too late.

Chapter 13
Fall Disaster

It was a beautiful day with The sun shining and the temperatures well above average for early November. Ellery and Madison were happy to be outside for school. Tomorrow, Madison was going to the take the state standardized test at the high school and was a little nervous. She had seen some of her close friends after leaving the hospital, but hadn't been part of the school for almost two months.

The next morning Ellery wished her daughter good luck on her tests and reminded her she would do great. Madison got out of the car and was relieved to see her friends waiting for her. The test consisted of several different subjects and would take most of the day to complete.

Everyone was out enjoying the extremely warm November day, including Ellery. After dropping Madison off, she took a walk and did some shopping, but now it was time to head home. She was hoping to get some lessons done and enjoy some solitude on the patio.

She noticed the sky darkening and decided to hurry before she got caught in the downpour. Late fall storms were not unusual for this area. They usually lasted a few hours and then the sky would clear. Ellery was hopeful that there would still be time to sit on the patio for part of the day. Sooner than expected the skies released the rain, along with a lot of thunder and lightning. She rushed to shut windows.

David looked out the window and commented to his patient and assistant that it was really raining and blowing. He looked at the sky and saw it was not the typical darkness of a storm, it looked different. Hail began hitting the windows. He gave a nod to his assistant signaling to leave and have Marge listen to the weather. The assistant, returned a short time later to tell him there were no storm warnings at this time. David still had an uneasy feeling and that the report would soon change.

Madison was on her last test when she heard a clap of thunder. Startled by the sound, she, along with many students, jumped in their seats. The thunder became louder and the sky went from dark to an almost greenish color. She

172

had never seen a green sky before and thought it was beautiful. Before turning her attention back to the test, she noticed the test proctors at the door talking to someone in the hall. Madison thought this was very unusual during standardized testing. She scolded herself for being distracted from the test.

David postponed starting on his next patient as he told Marge and the office staff to be prepared. He wanted all procedures to finish or not start. If they were at a good stopping point, don't proceed further. He was almost certain they would need to seek shelter quickly.

The weather report changed and Marge announced a strong tornado was headed towards them and to seek shelter now. David's building had a lower level that housed medical offices, so he and his staff assisted patients downstairs and into the designated shelters. Since David had given the directive not to start any new procedures, they were all able to leave immediately. Marge had thought to grab a box of masks so patients wouldn't breathe in air or dust, causing undue discomfort or possible infections. The medical staff brought in bottled water and blankets.

Ellery noticed that the storm seemed to settle into a calm and almost eerie feel, but pushed that feeling out of her mind. *Nothing like a good rain to cool things off. She gathered her teaching materials and sat at the kitchen table. It's not the patio, but it's still peaceful. Is that an ambulance siren? It sounds different.* She looked out the window and this time realized the green sky and eeriness meant a tornado forming. She quickly grabbed her cell phone and school items off the table and headed to the basement. Going down the steps she thought of Madison and David and prayed they would be safe.

Turning on the television she listened to the report. A tornado was in the area and everyone should seek shelter. She was thankful the family room had everything she needed; blankets, water, and a portable battery-operated radio.

The students began looking at each other when the school's tornado alarm sounded. *They would never schedule a drill during testing, so is this for real?* Madison could see through the windows that the storm had eased somewhat, so why the alarm? The teachers quickly directed the students to close their test booklets and follow protocol. Madison found one of her friends as she took her place in the hallway with the other students.

Protocol meant, knell with face to the wall, head down, and arms over your head. She had practiced this since kindergarten, but never had to do it for real. The announcement said it all – "This is not a drill. Please follow all protocols and listen to your teachers."

Madison looked around at the other students and then at her friend. She was afraid and also saw fear in so many other eyes she connected with. She silently prayed for protection.

Ellery couldn't get Madison out of her mind, to the point of near panic. Madison wasn't allowed a cell phone in the testing room, so there was no way to contact her. She knew the school only had hallways for a shelter. Tornados were rare in their area and she couldn't remember ever having one in November. She could hear what sounded like a continuous roll of thunder in the distance. Ellery decided to call David.

"David, are you okay?"

"Yes. We're all in the shelter. How about you and Madison? In the basement, I hope."

"I'm in the basement, but Madison is at the high school. She had testing today." Ellery said, her voice shaking.

David was trying to stay calm. He had been listening to the weather reports and it was a bad one. "I'm sure the school has her in a safe location and are taking care of things. There's nothing we can do, except pray for everyone's safety. She'll call when she can."

"She doesn't have her cell phone. They take them until the test is over." Ellery was explaining as the sound she had heard in the distance grew closer. It now sounded like a train or roaring jet engine. It was a horrible sound overhead. The house started to shake. "David! The house is shak…"

"Ellery? Ellery!" David tried several times to hear her answer. The line went dead and David was left with the unknown; helpless. He had heard the terrible sounds over the phone and knew Ellery was in danger. He couldn't go out in the storm because it was too severe and he had a responsibility to his staff and patients. Yet, he couldn't help but think what might be going on at home and at the school.

"Is everything okay, Dr. Weber?" Marge, asked.

"I pray so. I was talking with Ellery and she said something about the house and then the phone went dead."

Marge was always the one to try and keep everyone calm. "It's probably just the service being interrupted because of the storm. This will be over soon and then you head home. We can handle the office."

"Thank you, Marge." David said.

Inside the school, staff and students stayed huddled in the hallways, listening to the sounds from outside. They heard glass breaking inside the testing room. It sounded like someone was trying to break down the doors by ripping them off their hinges. Madison and her friend locked arms while still covering their heads at the same time. "This is the real thing." Madison said. "I hope it ends soon." Her friend nodded in agreement.

All of a sudden, the roof started shaking; darkness and screams followed. Staff yelling commands as they raced to help protect them. One teacher yelled, "Keep low! Cover your heads!" Then, like a tin can being ripped open, the roof abruptly flew off. Madison and others winced as debris fell on them.

Within minutes it was over. The all clear was announced and students were allowed to sit up with backs against the wall. Staff explained there was broken glass and debris on the ground, in addition to possible structural damage. Students were told to remain calm and stay put. Teachers walked up and down the hallway checking to make sure no one needed any medical attention. Madison wondered how students in the other parts of the building faired. She thought about her mom and dad, and if they were safe.

Marge announced the worst was over according to the radio. The staff began to help patients off the floor. David, and a few others, went to see if it was safe to leave the shelter. After a thorough check, they assisted patients back to the offices. Marge put the news on over the intercom system so all could hear the reports about the tornado.

The building had lost power and suffered some broken windows, along with losing a few shingles, but nothing serious given the force of the storm. The parking lot was a mess. Two cars were turned on their sides and some had broken windows. David's car had a cracked window, but no major damage. He had been spared.

David lived only five minutes away. He told Marge he was going to check on Ellery, but would call the office with any news. He hadn't heard anything about the high school and prayed he wouldn't. The police stopped him a few blocks from his house and asked if he lived in the area. They instructed him that all the power had been turned off, so down lines should be safe, but cautioned him to be careful. He was told that it may be necessary to walk part of the way, because some streets were blocked with large objects and fallen trees.

Driving down the street, David saw house after house with roofs off, walls missing, and cars overturned. The officer was correct. David couldn't go any further, so he parked the car and began to walk. He could see in the distance his house. He broke into a cold sweat, heart racing and mind fearing the worst. His brisk walk suddenly changed into a full out run, as if a runner who was sprinting to the finish line.

The visual sight was unnerving as he scanned for Ellery. He saw the garage was gone and her car upside down in the street. The roof were missing, exposing the entire second floor. Still, there was no sign of Ellery. As he got closer, he saw the front window in the living room was broken and the kitchen walls were missing. Breathing almost came to a complete stop as his eyes searched for his wife.

"Ellery! Ellery!" David yelled as he reached where the garage once stood. He continued towards the basement door, when he heard Ellery's voice.

"David!" Ellery was pounding on the door. "I can't open the door."

"There's something in front of it. It will take me a few minutes to clear it, so hang in there." David frantically worked, pushing and throwing debris aside. Finally he was able to force the door open. Ellery fell into his arms, relieved to see him and be out of her dark prison.

She looked at him and asked, "Madison?"

"I haven't heard anything on the radio about the high school, yet. We can try and get to the school if you want."

"Yes!"

Outside, Ellery couldn't believe what she saw. "Our house! The neighborhood is in shambles! Is that my car in the street?" Her legs turned to rubber. "Oh, David, what do we do now?"

David grabbed hold of her arm and pulled her away from the house and towards the car. "Now, we find our daughter."

Thinking ahead David told Ellery he would call the insurance company after they found Madison. "I'm sure they are swamped with calls right now. Also, after we make sure Madison is alright, you make hotel reservations for the next week. You may have to go outside the area, as I'm sure many rooms will be booked quickly."

Only two more blocks to the school entrance, but emergency vehicles stopped them from going through. They could see parents running towards the building. The police instructed David to park where he wouldn't block traffic and walk the rest of the way. They joined the pack of parents running and followed the frantic mob to the main entrance. It was here where all the parents stopped and fearfully waited for assistance. David had never before witnessed so much anxiety.

Someone with a megaphone was shouting instructions. Parents started moving and forming lines. David saw the line they needed to stand in and without saying a word, pushed Ellery towards the line.

"Child's name?" Mr. Allen, one of the school counselors, asked.

"Weber. Madison Weber."

"I don't see a Madison Weber on our roster." Mr. Allen said.

"She was here for testing. She's not a student here this semester." Ellery informed him and then nervously added, "Were there any injuries?"

Mr. Allen immediately reassured them. "Put your worries to rest. No serious injuries, just a few cuts and bruises. The building, however, was not so lucky. School may be closed for a while. Let me get someone to locate Madison."

They let out a long sigh of relief.

It didn't take long for Mr. Allen to get a response. "Someone is escorting her here. If you wouldn't mind waiting over there until she arrives, so we can keep the line moving, that would be appreciated."

"No problem and thank you." David said.

Within a few minutes, Madison appeared. After hugs, the three of them started for the car. David stopped them while he called the insurance company and his office. Ellery quickly looked up a few hotels nearby. Madison looked at them not understanding.

"Steve will be out tomorrow around eleven. How did you do?" David said.

"I found a room at the Embassy Suites about twenty minutes from here." Ellery reported. "We can go home and see if there is anything we can take with us."

"Wait, what you guys talking about? Who is Steve and why are we staying at the Embassy Suites?" Madison asked.

Her parents explained their house took a bad hit from the tornado. Not a complete loss, but a lot of damage.

Madison was shocked seeing the first houses in their neighborhood and then stood in disbelief in front of their house. She looked up to the second floor and saw no roof. All of the things in her room were either gone, strewn about, or damaged from the rain. She knew many of her paintings were gone. The few inside her dresser drawer may have been saved, but she wasn't counting on it.

David talked to one of the officers nearby, and came back to report that not only was the second floor unsafe, but the entire house was. "Let's head to the hotel and check in. Hopefully there will be a few stores near the hotel to get come clothes and other essentials."

"Not good news, but, we're all safe. Let's go." Ellery said.

They knew it would take several months to make the repairs on the house, so the next week was spent locating temporary housing and purchasing what they needed. They found a furnished apartment to rent and signed a short-term lease.

It took almost a year, but the house was finished. They were happy to be home in time for the holiday season, which was fast approaching.

Chapter 14
Unselfish Compassion

All the Christmas holiday activities were finally over. Eleanor was tired. She had overdone with volunteering and attending events and was now paying the price with a cold. But, before she could take a rest, there were a few more commitments to take care of. She promised the gallery two paintings by tomorrow and she had to mat and frame three photographs for shipping. The thought of what had to be done was in itself exhausting. Eleanor decided to take a few minutes and rest on her patio, however the few minutes turned into an hour.

Waking from her long nap, she presumed that she'd feel better, but no such luck. Her throat was getting scratchy and her head felt like someone was using a jackhammer inside it.

She struggled to get the energy to wrap the paintings up for the gallery. Tomorrow, she would get an early start and then call it a day. She knew rest was in order if there was to be any hope in stopping the cold from getting worse.

Pictures wrapped, Eleanor took some cold medicine and laid down. She didn't wake up until evening. Thinking she felt a little better, she headed to the studio to get the matting done. The three pictures were different sizes, so measuring and cutting each one separately was time consuming. Relieved the matting was done, Eleanor grabbed a cool drink, praying it would soothe her aching and scratchy throat.

Morning found her coughing and sneezing. Her nose and head were stuffy, and the pounding in her head was back. She took something for her headache, but not wanting to be drowsy for the drive into town, waited on the cold medicine. It didn't take long at the gallery, for which she was thankful. The owner noticed her pale color and suggested she go home and straight into bed. She couldn't agree more.

Eleanor stopped at the store to get juice, more cold medicine and a sandwich for lunch. After taking the medicine she went to the patio to enjoy the fresh air and rest. She did more than rest. Once again, she slept for several hours. *I should feel better after a long nap, but I don't. This is going to be a persistent cold. I can tell.*

Nourishment was in order, so with her sandwich and hot tea, she returned to the patio. Her throat continued to be sore and the coughing was no better. After eating half the sandwich, she went to the studio and finished preparing the photos. She had to get these shipped tomorrow and then she was done with all her commitments for a while. *Tomorrow I can sleep all day.*

Photographs loaded, she started for the post office. It wasn't too far into town, so she hoped to get there and home within an hour. *I can't believe that I feel worse after getting some sleep. I'd be okay with feeling the same. Here's the post office. I guess it's time to drag myself out of the car.* The young man behind the counter asked if she was alright. She told him it was just a cold and he wished her a speedy recovery. Looking in the mirror she understood why he had asked about her health.

Taking more medicine, getting a bottle of water, and making sure her bag of cough drops were close by, Eleanor crawled into bed. She was not simply tired; she was exhausted, yet restless. She couldn't sleep, so on came the television hoping the noise would help her relax more. It did somewhat, but the constant coughing kept her awake. Her chest hurt and felt heavy.

I just can't get a handle on this cold. I'm wiped out. It hurts to breathe. I'm coughing non-stop; my throat is a piece of sandpaper and my head is on fire and throbbing. Picking up the phone, she called to make an appointment with her doctor. She was surprised when they told her to come in immediately.

Dr. Carlos Diaz took one look at Eleanor and concerned crossed over his face. "My dear lady, you are very ill. I wish you would have come in sooner."

"I really thought it was just a bad cold." Eleanor said.

Peering over his glasses, he responded. "Well, we will know more after some x-rays, but I suspect pneumonia."

Eleanor waited in the examination room for the results of her x-rays, waiting for the doctor to come in. Finally, after some time, Dr. Diaz came into the room.

"I've looked at your x-rays and blood work, and along with my examination, you need to be in the hospital for a several days." Dr. Diaz said.

"The hospital?" Eleanor exclaimed. "Is that really necessary? I could just rest at home."

"Many times, I recommend that, but in your case, no. You are dehydrated and run down on top of the pneumonia. You need fluids and constant care for a few days. It is best for a safe and complete recovery. Your age factors into my decision, also." He said.

"Okay. I'll head straight there when I leave here." Eleanor stated.

"No. You need to call someone to pick you up and drive you to the hospital. Your car will be okay here in the parking lot or you can have a friend take it back to your house later." Dr. Diaz was a no-nonsense physician. "Do you have someone you can call, or do we take you by ambulance?"

This was the first time Eleanor realized she was worse than she had imagined. "I can call one of my neighbors to come get me."

"Good. Until they get here, I want you to rest. I mean, actually lay down on the exam table and rest. I will have the nurse bring in a blanket and pillow. When your ride gets here, we will come and get you. Understood?" Dr. Diaz was very blunt.

"Yes, doctor. I understand and I'll be a good patient. I promise." She held up the scout sign. He laughed on his way out of the room.

Eleanor called Charlotte Rogers first, hoping she and her husband were home. "Hello, Charlotte?"

"Hi, Eleanor. We haven't seen you on the beach lately. How are you?" Charlotte asked.

"Well, worse than I thought. I'm at the doctor's office. He said I have pneumonia and need to spend a few days in the hospital." Eleanor told her.

"What? Are you okay? What can we do?" Charlotte asked.

"I thought I was, but now I'm not so sure. I have a huge favor to ask. He won't let me drive to the hospital, so I'm calling to see if you and Dan can take me."

"Of course. I'll get Dan and we'll head out in a few. You still go to Dr. Diaz, right? Is that where you are?" Charlotte asked.

Eleanor breathed a sigh of relief she had found a ride. "Yes. Just let them know at the front desk you're here for me. I'll leave my car here and see if Elian or Mateo can pick it up and drive it back to my condo."

"Don't worry about your car. We'll make all the arrangements. Say, do you want anything from your place? I'm more than happy to pack a bag for you. That is, after we get you into the hospital." Charlotte offered.

"You're a dear friend. I'll see you and Dan soon." Eleanor ended the call.

Charlotte and Dan got Eleanor checked in and stayed until she was in settled in her room. The list of Eleanor's items in hand, Charlotte said goodbye and told her not to worry. They would take care of her car, plants, mail, and also, keep an eye on her place.

Eleanor found her eyes closing before they even left the room. She drifted off to sleep, thanking God for so many good friends that helped fill the void in her life. Waking up later, she felt rested for the first time in days. She still had a persistent cough and breathing was difficult, but being cared for is what she needed. She wasn't even concerned about her home. For the first time in two weeks, she was completely relaxed.

Dr. Diaz stopped in to see Eleanor the next morning. "You look better already. Getting fluids into you and making sure you rest is making a big difference in your recovery."

"I hate to say this, but you were right. You were wise to have me in the hospital, because I would have found small projects to do at home."

"Looking at your chart, your temperature is back to normal and your other vital signs are good. I am hopeful that after two or three more days, you will be well enough to go home." Dr. Diaz said.

"That sounds great. How soon before I'm back to one hundred percent?".

"I can see it's going to be hard to hold you back. You must, and I emphasize, must, continue to rest. You may paint and read. No housework for a good week and no long walks on the beach. In fact, you need someone to be with you even for short walks." He cautioned.

"Any special diet? I've only had soft foods here and I seem to be hungry between meals. Like now."

"No special diet when you go home and I'll see they switch you to an unrestricted diet for the rest of your stay.

You may want to ask someone to prepare several meals for you before going home. No major cooking for a while. At least until you are stronger."

Dr. Diaz was very compassionate, but gave directions like a schoolmarm. Eleanor chuckled at the thought of Dr. Diaz in front of a class with chalk in hand instructing students on their lessons. *He's a great doctor and cares very much about all of his patients physical, mental, and economic states.*

Charlotte and Dan came later that morning with the things from Eleanor's list. She didn't need much for her short stay, but thought a few toiletries, Bible, and a book would be nice to have. Charlotte even thought to bring a light shawl, in case Eleanor became chilled. "It can't hurt to spruce up a drab hospital gown," she said.

Later in the day, Pastor Tony arrived bringing words of well wishes from the church and a beautiful bouquet of flowers from his wife, Juanita. He had been in contact with Charlotte and together they found volunteers to take care of the house cleaning, groceries, laundry, and any yard work. They also had a list of several people to come over for an hour or so to keep her company and prepare meals.

This was too much for Eleanor. In all her years she had never had such a loving group of people to give of themselves to her out of love. She wished she could somehow capture this on canvas. Compassionate people living the example of Christ, doing for others without expecting anything in return. Eleanor loved Pastor Harris and the congregation in the states, but this was different. The people here gave with a servant's heart, and not simply out of duty.

Eleanor was happy to be home and free from the confines of a hospital. Charlotte was out of town, so neighbors Grace and Maria made sure she got home. Walking into her house it was as though she had just walked into a greenhouse. Fragrant flowers and plants graced almost every room. The ladies had divided them between the bedroom, den, dining room, and patio, so no matter where she went, she had a plant or bouquet to enjoy. Eleanor looked at them and thought of the people and their unselfish love.

The ladies let Eleanor know that they had food delivered and labeled in the refrigerator, along with juices, water, and soft drinks. They gave her a list of who had volunteered to come on what days and what times, and if she wasn't up for company, let them know. If the name had a star next to it, the person was coming to clean or do whatever chores needed to be done.

Eleanor couldn't believe the organization behind this and the time it took to contact all these people. It was also overwhelming that so many people offered to just come and sit with her. "Thank you both, and everyone, so much. This is very humbling and appreciated. I think I will be fine for today, but I'm sure tomorrow a few visitors would be nice."

"You are welcome." Maria said. "Are you sure you don't need someone to come around dinner time to fix your meal? You may find yourself very tired by tonight."

"That is a smart idea. Eleanor laughed. "Yes, tonight, I would love someone to help. I think I can manage lunch, though."

"Lunch is already for you." Grace interjected. "It's in the refrigerator, top shelf. A salad and fruit. Rolls are on the counter."

"You both have thought of everything. Thank you so much. I know Charlotte had a lot to do with this, and will thank her when she returns. I'm sure many people have had their hand in preparing for my homecoming." Eleanor said.

"Yes. Quite a few people volunteered to help. Now, we will go and leave you to rest. Is there anything you need before we leave?" Grace asked.

"No. I'm good. I plan to sit here, watch television or read, and sip on this juice you brought me. I appreciate all of this so much."

"We don't want you to see us out. Stay put and get more rest. Someone will text you when it's time for dinner. See you later." Maria said, as both ladies left the room.

Chapter 15
The Unthinkable Happens

February was proving to be one of the coldest on record, and it didn't seem like it would get warmer any time soon. It was a quiet Sunday morning and Ellery was thankful all the repairs on the house were done.

She and David were going to a fiftieth wedding anniversary party tonight, and because it was over an hour away, they decided it was a good excuse to spend the night and drive back in the morning. Madison had returned to school at the start of the new semester, so she would spend the night with the Richardson's, close family friends.

It had been a busy weekend with ice skating, shopping, and now the party. Ellery was excited to get away, even if it was for just one night. They planned to leave within the hour, providing David finished packing the car and Ellery completed the final touches on the gift wrapping. She didn't relish the idea of going out in the cold multiple times during the next two days, but it's what you do every winter when you live in the north.

"Are you ready?" David asked, interrupting her thoughts.

"Yes. Present is wrapped and ready to take. Do we have time to stop for coffee on the way?" Ellery hoped the answer would be yes.

"We have plenty of time. The party isn't until 4 p.m. We even have time for a quick lunch when we get there." David said.

"Sounds perfect. Let's go." Ellery slipped on her coat.

It was a beautiful day, except for the cold. The sun shone through the car windows, warming them like a bun in a toaster oven. The roads were fairly clear of traffic. David and Ellery talked and laughed, and at times rode in silence; each in their own thoughts. Music played softly on the radio.

Madison and Angela went ice skating for most of the afternoon. They spent equal amounts of time on the ice and in the lodge. By the time Kathy picked them up, they looked like polar bears, all covered with snow that fell quickly off as they got into the car. Kathy turned the heat on high as she gave them blankets and two cups of hot chocolate.

"Thanks, Mrs. Richardson." Madison said, as her teeth chattered loudly.

"Ditto that," Angela added.

"You are welcome. How was skating?" Kathy asked.

"Great!" They answered in unison. Madison added, "It was almost too cold, but we went into the lodge a lot to keep warm."

"Good to hear. You can watch a movie when we get home while I fix dinner. It's a school night so, it will be to bed early." Kathy told them.

"Okay, Mom. We have a test in chemistry, so we're going to study a little tonight, too." Angela said.

The Richardson's had been friends with the Weber's for many years and sleepovers were a common event in both households. Ellery was at peace knowing Madison would be well taken care of by a family that considered her a second daughter.

David and Ellery reached the party ahead of schedule. They parked the car and walked to a small diner. They spent time talking about their future plans, their hopes and dreams for Madison, and their continued search for Eleanor. It felt good to sit and talk together with no interruptions.

The dinner was absolutely perfect. Everyone was happy and the couple was pleased so many had come. They had been close friends of David's parents and David adored them. Ellery could tell that being here made David miss his parents. His dad passed away when David was a teenager and his mom died of pneumonia when he was in his twenties.

They wished the couple another fifty years and left for their hotel. It was still early, so they decided to take advantage of the amenities. The indoor heated pool was perfect to get the body moving after riding and sitting for most of the day. The hot tub was exactly what the they needed to complete their relaxation. They planned to call it a night after leaving the hot tub, until David declared he was starving.

"It may sound strange, but so am I," Ellery replied.

"Well, we can go out and find someplace that's open, go down to the hotel restaurant, or order room service." David proposed.

"I vote for room service." Ellery said. "I'm too relaxed to move from this room." David quickly agreed.

They ordered an appetizer tray, the restaurant's special chocolate cake, and of course, a pot of coffee. It was a glorious evening they both had desperately needed. Time away and time together. They stayed up for hours talking and laughing before collapsing into a deep sleep.

Madison and Angela reviewed for their chemistry test. They both felt prepared and ready to tackle any question the teacher threw at them. Kathy came in to say goodnight and that she would wake them up early. This would give them more than enough time to go to their lockers and visit with friends before school started.

David and Ellery slept in for the first time in years. There was no work, church, school, or any other activities that had to get them out of bed early. David suggested to enjoy a leisurely breakfast before heading home. Opening the drapes, Ellery noticed it had snowed during the night and there was a light snow still falling. Getting an early start would let them be home before Madison got out of school.

Leaving the hotel, after stuffing themselves with waffles, muffins, and coffee, they started the few hours to home. It had been a wonderful two days, but it was time to get back. The roads were lightly covered with. David assured Ellery that the roads weren't slippery, just snow covered. Ellery sat back to enjoy the ride and conversation.

As they were rounding a curve, David noticed a truck out of control and heading straight for them. He tried to maneuver the car to safety, but the truck veered and hit them almost head on. It sent the car flipping several times before landing in the field.

Everything was blurry as Ellery tried to focus. She saw David. He wasn't moving. She couldn't reach him. Her body was frozen. Ellery thought she could hear people yelling and tried to answer, but all went dark. It took time to get Ellery out of the car so paramedics could work on her. By then, she was in a coma. The ambulance sped towards the hospital as emergency workers stayed at the scene. The two people in the truck had been killed instantly. David had no chance of surviving such an impact and was pronounced dead at the scene, also. The police found that the truck driver lived in the area and had a wife and two children. They soon located Ellery's purse and had the information needed to begin the search for a relative. The computer base listed a daughter.

Police were soon at the high school asking to see the principal. Mrs. Cavanaugh, the school secretary, took the two officers to see Principal Havensworth.

"Mr. Havensworth, I'm Officer Cabot. Do you have a Madison Weber at this school and is she here today?"

Mr. Havensworth confirmed that Madison Weber was a current student and was in attendance today.

"Mr. and Mrs. Weber have been in a severe accident and I'm afraid it's not good news. Officer Cabot paused to allow Mr. Havensworth to process the news. "Are there any relatives that could come to the school? It might be best if they are here when Madison is told."

"No relatives that live close. However, Madison is staying with the Richardson's." Mr. Havensworth said.

"Thank you," the officer said. "These are never easy calls, especially when children are involved.

"Hello, Kathy?" Mr. Havensworth, asked.

"Yes," Kathy responded.

"This is Principal Havensworth at the high school. This call is in regards to Madison. There has been an accident involving her parents. Are you able to come to school?"

Kathy grew weak and began to shake. "Yes. I'll be right there." She placed a call to her husband as she grabbed her purse and coat and headed out the door. Sitting in the car, she told him about the phone call and breathed a sigh of relief when he said he could leave immediately and meet her at the school. The call finished, she started for the school. Kathy prayed as she drove, while at the same time envisioning everything from a minor accident to the worse.

Mrs. Cavanaugh showed Kathy to the principal's office. Kathy told her that she was expecting her husband, Craig, at any time and to please have him join her. Mrs. Cavanaugh nodded and went back to the front desk, not yet knowing what this was all about. She just knew it was something bad, but what she didn't realize was how bad and for a different student.

As Kathy was getting seated, Craig entered the room and took the chair next to his wife. He nodded at the principal, who looked thankful to see him.

Mr. Havensworth got right to the point. "I'm glad you are both here. Madison's parents have been in a very bad accident about seventy-five miles from here. They were on their way home when an oncoming pickup truck lost control and hit the Weber's car almost head-on."

Kathy gasped. She knew what a head-on collision meant. Craig took her hand. "Please. Go on."

"Officer Cabot can fill you in on the details, but I am very sorry to inform you that David was killed immediately and Ellery is in critical condition."

"No! This can't be!" Kathy cried out. "We were going to have dinner tonight. Madison is back in school and doing well. This just can't be. This must be a mistake?"

Craig wrapped his arms around his wife, knowing at this moment he must remain strong. Softly he spoke to her and then to Officer Cabot. "Please tell us what you know."

Officer Cabot began. "As Mr. Havensworth said, an oncoming pickup truck lost control coming around a curve. The Weber's car was hit, primarily on the driver's side and then rolled several times. The two people in the truck and Mr. Weber were killed instantly. Mrs. Weber is in a coma and in critical condition.

"Madison is in class and hasn't been told anything. I wanted someone close to her, to be here when she hears the news." The principal added.

"Thank you for thinking of her," Craig said. "Should Angela be here when we tell Madison?"

"I think it's best if Angela goes to the counselor's office and is told there. We can do that first and let her have some time to compose herself before we tell Madison," the principal said.

"That's a good idea," Craig said.

Mr. Havensworth called the counselor, Ms. Jackson, to his office along with Mrs. Cavanaugh. He wanted the two ladies to be in the counseling office when Mr. Richardson told his daughter about the Weber's. Craig took this time to ask the name of the hospital Ellery was taken to from Office Cabot, before he left.

"Hello, Madison. Won't you sit down?" Principal Havensworth said.

Madison looked around and saw Mr. and Mrs. Richardson in the room. She knew something was wrong, but nothing could prepare her for what she was about to hear.

Craig sat next to Madison and spoke very gently and compassionately. "Madison, there has been an accident involving your parents."

"Accident? Where?"

"About an hour from here. A truck came around a curve and lost control. It hit your parent's car. Your mom is in critical condition and your dad . . . I'm so sorry Madison . . . your dad... he didn't make it. He was killed instantly." Craig told her.

"No! No! It's not true!" Madison yelled out. Kathy held her as she broke into loud sobs as the news sunk in. Craig thought telling Angela was difficult, but it was nothing compared to telling Madison.

It took some time before Madison began to calm down before she asked, "Can I go see my mom? I want to see her. Please?"

"We will go as soon as we can. You need to pack a few things. You and Mrs. Richardson will be spending the night, maybe a few nights, near the hospital. Think you can do that, sweetie?" Craig said.

Mr. Havensworth buzzed the counselor's office and asked that Ms. Jackson escort Angela to his office. Mrs. Cavanaugh, Ms. Jackson, and Angela all walked into the office with red eyes. Angela went to her friend and they hugged tightly as each shed more tears. A few minutes later, they left. Craig thanked the school staff and said he would be in touch after he knew more.

Kathy took Madison to her house and waited in the living room while Angela helped Madison pack her bag. Kathy looked around and thought back to all the parties, dinners, and vacations the two families had shared. It was now changed, forever. As the girls returned, Madison stopped and took the recent family picture off the mantle. "Mom will want this in her room."

"That's a lovely thought. I'm sure it will comfort her. Mr. Richardson is meeting us at home and then he'll drive us to the hospital." Kathy told her. "Angela will ride with us to the hospital, but she won't be staying.

At the hospital, Madison slowly went into her mother's room. She had been told her mom was in pretty bad shape and not to be surprised or upset with all the equipment in the room. She saw her mom lying still, so very still. Her face was badly bruised and there were so many tubes and machines.

"Mom? It's Madison. You're going to be okay. You just need some rest."

There was no response from Ellery.

Madison pulled up the chair, took her mom's hand and laid her head down and wept. The Richardson's waited outside giving Madison private time alone with her mom. They were comforted that a nurse was just inside the door, if Madison needed someone. After several minutes, the nurse quietly told Madison that her mom needed to rest, but she could come back later. Kathy was then allowed to go in for just a few minutes to see Ellery.

"I want to see my dad." Madison told Mr. Richardson. He looked skeptical and tried to talk her out of it, but Madison insisted. "Please. I have to say goodbye. It's my last chance to say goodbye."

"Okay. Let me get it arranged." Craig returned with the doctor who took them to the room. Angela stayed in the hallway while the doctor led the others into the room where David's body lay.

There were no words, only silent tears. The three stood back to allow Madison some privacy. Craig held his wife, knowing this was going to be hard on her, as well as Madison. He thought about the arrangements that needed to be made. Ellery was unable and Madison was too young to have that responsibility put on her. He would talk with the doctor in private, later.

"Dad. Oh, Dad. I love you… I don't know what I'll do without you. You were my buddy. Mom isn't able to say goodbye yet. She doesn't even know!... What am I going to do?... How will Mom and I make it without you?... What's going to happen?" Madison's heart was breaking.

Kathy could hardly stand to watch as Madison tried to say goodbye to her father. The questions Madison asked were similar to the ones she was asking herself. *Now what? How will Madison take care of her mom? Ellery will be in the hospital for a long time and then, according to the doctor, she will be in rehab for several more months. Ellery will need Madison near her.*

Craig had called David's sister shortly after leaving the school and gave her all the information he had. She would be on the next flight out. He then called their pastor and David's office. The calls he made were the hardest calls he's ever had to do. He thought it would get easier with each call, but it didn't. Craig hoped Kristin and Madison would be available to give him some direction with the decisions that needed to be made.

Angela was ready to hug Madison goodbye when her father suggested she stay for a few days, too. Angela turned and hugged her dad, as did Madison. Craig and Kathy looked at each other knowing this was the right decision, to allow Angela to stay. Kathy had secretly packed for Angela, just on the off chance they decided to let her stay.

Craig dropped the three off at the hotel, a block from the hospital, and headed home. Kathy had gotten a suite which allowed them more amenities and plenty of room to relax. She hoped Madison would soon be able to relax and also get a good night's sleep. It was hard for her to see Ellery fighting for her life, not to mention David's lifeless body. She could only imagine the torment Madison was going through.

Chapter 16
God's Special Angel

Four weeks had gone by and Ellery was still in the hospital. She came out of the coma a few days after the accident and was told that David had been killed. Kristin was there to grieve with her. Ellery's heart ached for David and the pain only deepened knowing she wasn't able to see him or even say goodbye. Only the memories left, including the special memories of their last two days together.

Kristin stayed with Madison after Kathy and Angela left, but she it was time for her to go home. There was still much to do, such as Ellery's recovery, burial arrangements, and helping Madison navigate through all of this. Before Kristin left, arrangements had to be made for Madison to stay with someone. She was a retired missionary from one of the area churches willing to open her home to Madison for as long as needed.

Iris Swanson was the sister of a member from Madison's church. She was thrilled to help and excited to have a young person in her home. Iris had been a missionary for thirty years in Peru. She loved her mission work, but found as she got older, it was too hard to live in the mountains and travel from village to village. She returned to her home town and stayed active in the church. She lived alone in a small two-bedroom house not far from the hospital. It was perfect for Madison.

Madison was somewhat reluctant to stay with a stranger, so her Aunt Kristin stayed a few days longer to help her adjust to the change. She and Madison helped Iris around the house, and learned the way to the hospital and grocery store. By the time Kristin left, Madison was at ease with her new living arrangements. Iris encouraged Madison to make this her temporary home and invite her friends over to visit, bake, rearrange furniture, or just spend time painting.

Ellery was doing better, but still had several months of physical therapy ahead of her. The doctors explained with therapy, hard work, and time she should go from wheelchair to walker, and then hopefully to a cane, but they made it clear there were no guarantees. Her goal was to be out of the wheelchair by summer. The Richardson's came almost every weekend, giving Madison some normal time away from the hospital. Ellery was well taken care of and was so appreciative of everyone who had come to her aid. She was even more grateful for the care and love everyone was giving to Madison. Her heart still longed for David.

Madison went back to being homeschooled. She missed all the activities and challenges of her old school, but homeschool allowed her to go at a faster or slower pace, depending on her needs. But, most importantly, it let her stay close to her mom. Iris had been a teacher for many years at a mission school in Peru. She loved teaching and Madison was an excellent student. She encouraged Madison to continue with her painting and asked an art teacher from church to give her art lessons once a week.

Ellery was now well enough to be transferred to a rehab facility closer to home. Iris offered to stay with Madison until Ellery was able to be discharged, which was a big relief for Ellery. The arrangement for David's funeral was scheduled for the first week in April. Approval for Ellery to attend the funeral was given, providing she was accompanied by a health care aide and she didn't overdo.

Emotions of sadness and joy were all mixed together on the day of the funeral. Ellery felt a constant sting of sadness in her heart. She was burying the love of her life without being able to say goodbye, hold his hand or touch his face one last time. But, she couldn't dwell on that. God had spared her so she could take care of their daughter and David was safe in Heaven. Even knowing this, the sting and enormous grief was still there.

Madison had said her goodbyes months ago and was now being asked to relive it again. Her mind, heart, and stomach were all twisted in knots, but the focus was to be strong for her mom. Plagued with the thought that her father's death could have somehow been punishment for her plot against her gramma was only lessened by Angela. Her friend was there for her, by her side all day.

Pitying eyes would cast a shadow over Madison, causing her to seek refuge wherever she could. Angela made the whole ordeal easier by pulling her into a closet or behind a tree, anywhere to be free from the eyes. Every so often, laughter would emerge when Angela would mock the way someone looked, the hideous outfit they wore, or the way they talked. Madison knew this wasn't nice to do, but it helped ease the tension and sadness of the day.

Ellery was getting pretty good at maneuvering her wheelchair. At rehab, she was learning how to adapt to life at home without assistance. She could then be discharged and return only for her outpatient physical therapy. Ellery worked hard and improved each day. She wanted to be home with Madison. No, she needed to be home with Madison.

She longed to be her teacher but most importantly, be the parent Madison so desperately needed.

Iris loved this family. It wasn't a burden to stay and continue to help them. She wanted to assist in any way she could. For her, it fulfilled a void in her life. A life she lived through serving and teaching.

Ellery prayed she would have enough energy to do everything she wanted to do. She still wondered why God allowed this to happen. He had a reason, she knew, but it was hard sometimes to accept what happened and not know the why.

Discharge day finally arrived. Ellery was going home and Madison was thrilled. Madison and Iris had been working all week preparing the house for the homecoming. Church members built ramps and made the house wheelchair accessible.

Iris and Madison made minor revisions in the kitchen by moving plates and cooking utensils to lower shelves. They also moved furniture so the wheelchair could maneuver easily. The house was ready and so was Ellery.

It was an adjustment to be home, but Ellery wouldn't change it for anything. She and Madison spent time together, whether it was schooling, gardening, or playing games. Iris was considered part of the family and was included in all activities. Iris and Ellery enjoyed sharing the teaching.

The three soon established a routine for daily duties, schooling and therapy. On physical therapy days, Iris would drop Ellery off at the rehab center and Madison at her destination before visiting her sister, who lived within a few miles of the rehab center. If Madison didn't have art or music, she would sit in the rehab center's cafeteria and do her other studies. It was during these times that she began thinking about her future schooling options.

Madison expressed her ideas with her mom and Iris and then made an appointment for them to speak with Principal Havensworth. Madison was getting ready to enter her junior year and wanted to go back to school, but still be at home to help. She had worked out a plan and hoped the principal would approve.

"Welcome, ladies. What is it you want to discuss?" Mr. Havensworth asked.

"Madison has some ideas about her education that she wants to talk about, Mr. Havensworth." Ellery replied.

Madison took a deep breath before speaking. "Thank you for being willing to meet with us. I would typically meet with the counselor about next year, but my situation is a bit different. I miss being at school and participating in all the activities, but I also want to continue with homeschooling and help take care of my mom." She took a slight pause, cleared her throat and continued.

"I have thought this through in detail, and here is what I propose. I would like to take math and science here at the high school in the morning and then be homeschooled for the remainder of my subjects. Madison, eyes hopeful, looked at the principal before asking, "What do you think? Is it possible?"

Mr. Havensworth took time before responding. "Given your unique circumstance, I think we may be able to work it out. We need to talk to your counselor and schedule your classes for the first two hours of the day. What are you going to do about electives? I ask because, if you want to walk with your class at graduation, which because of your unique situation, I will allow, you still must meet all the requirements."

Madison smiled broadly. "Thank you. I really do want to take part in graduation. I thought I could take two college classes either at the local community college or online. I also want to take art and voice lessons once a week. I can go over it with the counselor and get her approval for dual enrollment before I make a decision."

"You have thought this through in great detail. I believe it might work," Principal Havensworth said. "What do you think, Mrs. Weber?"

Ellery couldn't help but smile. "I believe my daughter has thought this out thoroughly also, and I like the plan. We will talk about the electives and how all of this will work with schedules. Ms. Swanson will be leaving before next school year, so I will be doing the other subjects."

"I will be leaving, that's true, but I'm only a FaceTime call away. I just love technology, even at my age." Iris laughed before continuing on. "I do have one question. Madison mentioned to me, and I think has forgotten to ask, is she able to take driver's education?"

"Driver's education is a four-week course held after school. However, we do have a summer program, if that would be better. I will see if there is room in the morning class." Mr. Havensworth said.

Madison said she preferred to take it during the summer, leaving the school year for studies and helping her mom. She looked at her mom and Iris, who nodded their approval. Mr. Havensworth said he would contact the teacher and let them know.

Before they left, Mr. Havensworth scheduled a time for Madison to meet with the counselor before the school year was over. He told Madison and Ellery that he would talk with Ms. Jackson before the meeting so she understood what the plan was and to have some suggestions for college classes.

Ellery was gaining strength and beginning to use a walker during therapy. She knew if she kept working hard, the wheelchair would be a thing of the past, even at home.

The day finally came when her therapist told her she was ready to retire the wheelchair. Cheers erupted as Ellery surprised Madison and Iris when she entered the room using a walker. A celebration was in order, Iris announced. After stuffing themselves at the restaurant, they spent the night watching movies, talking, laughing, and eating the dessert they couldn't quite finish at dinner.

A few days later, Madison asked her mom if they could start searching for Gramma again. The search had been on hold for too long, and Madison wanted to find her now more than ever. Iris was ready and willing to help in any way she could.

At first, searching was slow, as they reviewed what they already knew and made plans on where to look next. They had called Eleanor's realty office when David was still alive and had simply been told the realtor was no longer with them. Iris wanted to give it another try. Speaking with the office manager, she asked if there were any notes that could be shared, as it pertained to a missing family member. She mentioned that there had been a tragedy in the family. She learned that Eleanor was indeed a client of Lakeshore Realty, and notes showed she had moved somewhere in the Virgin Islands, but no specifics were given.

This was the best news Ellery and Madison had gotten in a very long time. They couldn't thank Iris enough for helping them. Iris had spent a lot of time searching for missing children in Peru and had learned different ways to get information. Now came the tedious job of going through the checklist, island by island. This would take some time, but at least the area had been narrowed down, providing Eleanor hadn't moved again, or worse, died.

Chapter 17
Fleeing the Storm

The island was bracing for a possible category-3 hurricane by the end of the week. Residents were being advised, especially along the coast, to secure their homes and property, and then leave within the next four days. Eleanor was busy preparing her home for the worst. She was glad for the hurricane shutters, which made it easier to secure the outside, and hoped they would stand up against the storm. A storm she had never before witnessed first-hand.

She spent the last few days reading and re-reading the brochure on preparing for a hurricane, but it didn't ease her mind much. She tested the shutters a few months ago and was amazed at how easy it was to close and fasten them by herself. She would secure them tomorrow.

Eleanor decided to take her art work to the gallery for safe storage. Even though somewhat costly, it was the best option. With the task of protecting her work finally done, she turned her concentration to packing everything she thought might be needed. Her dining room table looked more like she was preparing for a major camping expedition. All that was missing were tents and guides. She hoped none of these items would be needed to survive, but, she was a planner, and the brochure made it clear to be prepared for anything. Her camera, considered non-essential by most, was extremely essential to her and was being packed with the rest of the items.

The storm, according to the news, was getting closer and possibly gaining in strength, but it was still too early to predict landfall. It was all so confusing looking at the many different colored lines leading from the hurricane to various points of possible impact. One of the lines was directed at her beach. She had been through some rough storms while living in St. Croix, but never a hurricane. Her only reference was from watching news reports over the years. This time, she was part of the news.

Listening to the latest report on the impending storm, she was troubled it was arriving earlier than scheduled. People were told to leave the coastal areas no later than 10 a.m. tomorrow and seek shelter inland. She went out to the patio and looked up and down the row of condos. About half of them still had lights on and the other half were dark. *There is no sense in cutting it close. I'll finish packing the car now and leave first thing in the morning,*

She awoke early and quickly packed the last-minute items in her car. The winds had picked up which made Eleanor thankful she had closed and locked all the hurricane shutters yesterday. Taking a last minute check, making sure everything was turned off inside the house, including the lights, she took a deep breath, climbed into her car and headed inland toward the shelters.

The wind and rain started to increase as she turned off her street. Turning on the radio she listened intently as the announcer was saying, "The storm is arriving even sooner than predicted. If you are on the road, find shelter soon." Eleanor wondered if she should return and wait out the storm in her condo or try and make it to one of the shelters. She decided to continue on and prayed that she would arrive to one in time. Driving through town she saw papers flying through the air, in a well-choreographed pattern. She noted a bit of chaos blowing around her as the dancing papers were no longer dancing, but were at war.

She headed along the coast for a few miles and then turned to go inland; hopefully away from the storm. Because of the heavy rain and winds, she had to go much slower than she wanted. A few miles down the road she spotted people up ahead. It was a man carrying a small child and a woman with a large bundle under her coat. *Why on earth would they be out in this?*

That man is waving frantically at cars and not one is stopping. They don't even slow down! I can't drive by and do nothing. She stopped the car and asked, "Do you need a ride?"

"Please. Yes." The man answered.

"Get in. There is room for everyone." It was then that Eleanor noticed the package was a baby. *A baby! Thank you Jesus for putting me on this road at this time.*

"Thank you. You sure you don't mind?" He said.

"Where else would you go? The storm is closing in and fast, according to the news."

He got his family and belongings in before jumping in the front seat. He turned to the back and quickly asked, "Are you and the children all settled, Maria?"

"We're fine. Angelica and I are a bit wet, but the baby's dry and quiet for now." She replied.

"Well," Eleanor said. "Time for introductions don't you think? I'm Eleanor Morgan and I'm headed to a shelter."

"I'm Juan Cruz, my wife, Maria, daughter, Angelica, and son, Diego." He wasn't a tall man, but she could tell he worked out. "We can't thank you enough for stopping. So many cars went by and didn't even slow down. I was starting to worry if I could keep my family safe."

Eleanor paused, as the winds were fighting to take control of the car, and the pounding rain made it difficult to see. "It's none of my business, but why are you walking with a hurricane almost upon us?"

"We don't have a car. We were told to get on one of the buses headed to a shelter. We walked four miles to the bus. When we got there, they said sorry, someone gave you the wrong advice, you can't take this bus. We didn't have time to go back to the apartment, so we decided to walk inland. I really thought someone would offer us a ride. The hurricane came faster than we prepared for." Juan said.

"That is just plain wrong." Eleanor huffed.

Eleanor looked around and saw the trees bending and swaying in all different directions. She now wondered whether they would make the shelter in time. The radio gave an update on the storm. "Get off the roads. Seek shelter wherever you are." She had no sense of where she was or how far the shelter was. They seemed to be the only car on the road. Looking ahead and side-to-side, she didn't see anywhere to seek cover.

The storm was getting worse and she hadn't seen a car for the last few minutes. She also knew they weren't inland enough and, worse yet, they were still in a low area of the island. Too low to be safe from any rising waters. She began to wonder if she had traveled too far south before turning inland. Maybe she should have stayed at the condo, but the last report said it was headed straight for her. Besides, where would Juan and Maria be if she hadn't taken this road?

A strange noise awakened her from her thoughts. It kept getting louder as they drove. Eleanor knew it wasn't the storm and glanced at Juan, who visibly had concern on his face. "Any idea what the noise is?"

He simply shook his head.

The car started sputtering and chugging. Knowing this wasn't a good sign, she looked for a place to pull over as soon as possible, and for any signs of shelter, but saw nothing. The houses in this area were all boarded up and no life was visible. The world seemed to be spinning around them and she wondered if they too would soon be spinning. Eleanor's hands tightened on the steering wheel as she kept driving. She and Juan knew finding shelter may be their only chance to survive.

"There! Up ahead. It looks like a building. Do you see it? It looks like it may still be under construction." Juan said.

Eleanor exclaimed, "Yes! I see it. Under construction or not, it's shelter." Just then the engine stopped. She let it coast as far as possible, hoping to get closer to the building. "Do you think all of us can make it?"

"Let me run ahead and make sure we can get in somehow. It's less than fifty yards." Juan offered.

"Sounds like a plan," Eleanor said. "Be careful."

They watched him struggle against the wind. He turned, and ran back trying to keep his balance. He found a way in. Juan told his wife that he would take their large backpack and Angelica, and she could take the baby. Eleanor grabbed her backpack, the tote with the flashlights, candles, and such, and her camera bag. She let them know she wouldn't be able to run, so not to wait for her. She assured them, though, she was a fast walker.

Thankful that she was weighted down, Eleanor fought the elements as she worked hard to reach the door. She remembered the old saying, one step forward and two steps back. Well today she realized it was more than a figure of speech.

The hotel was finished enough to provide safe shelter. Behind the bare front counter was a door; possibly an office. Juan quickly opened the door and got everyone inside just as they heard glass breaking. It was a perfect room. No windows, but it had several chairs and two desks to seek shelter under.

Juan said he would make a trip to the car and get as much as he could. Eleanor and Maria questioned if that was a good idea.

"If I go now, I can get the food and water before it's too late. Maria, watch for me and open the door when I'm close." Juan saw the fear in Maria's eyes and touched her cheek to let her know he would be alright before opening the door and subjecting himself to the will of the storm.

Maria watched him struggling and gasped as he fell. It took several minutes for him to gain control. He crawled a few feet at a time until he got closer to the building. As Juan approached, she pushed on the door. The force of the wind was against her, as she summoned every ounce of strength she had to push it open. She was making a little progress when the door suddenly broke off its hinges and propelled towards her, slamming her body against the wall.

Dropping the items, Juan yelled. "Maria! There was no response. "Maria!" He yelled again as he reached her.

Maria, slowly opened her eyes. "I'm okay. I think I just had the wind knocked out of me."

Eleanor, hearing the commotion, hurried over to them. "Juan, what happened?"

"The door let loose and knocked her against the wall." Juan was breathless. "Are you okay to stand? We need to move. It's not safe here."

"Yes." But, as Maria tried to stand, she slid back down and winced in pain.

"What is it?" Juan asked.

"My shoulder. It really hurts to move."

Juan and Eleanor helped her up and back to the office, being careful of her shoulder. Maria sat in the chair cradling her arm. "I think it's bruised and nothing more. I'll sit here for a few minutes to make sure. The children? Are they okay?"

"Diego is already asleep and Angelica is soon to follow." Eleanor pointed to the two children under one of the desks.

Juan, was still very concerned for his wife. "Are you sure you're okay?"

"Yes, Juan. Stop worrying so." Maria touched his arm trying to reassure him.

"If you're sure, I'll bring in the food and water. Then, I'll see about securing this door." Juan said.

"Maria. I'm curious what's behind this door. Any idea?" Maria shook her head no. With a twinkle in her eye, Eleanor opened the door and saw it led to a hallway. Glancing up and down, she saw a door, directly across from the office, that said Housekeeping. Peering inside she sent a quick thank you to God, as it was lightly stocked with linens, blankets, and pillows. Loading her arms with supplies, she returned to the office.

"It's not a lot, but it will help, especially the blankets. An early delivery must have been made. It was as if someone knew we were coming ahead of the hotel opening." Eleanor announced, setting the supplies on the desk. Without saying another word, she left to look in more rooms, even though she knew it wasn't the safest thing to do. She heard the winds outside pounding angrily, trying to force their way in. She tried another door close to the office. Jackpot. Four new mattresses, still wrapped, leaned against the wall.

Eleanor started pulling one of the mattresses out when she heard a loud crash. Leaving the mattress and rushing back into the office, she saw everyone was safe. Juan came in and said that one of the large windows in the lobby exploded.

"It's best we stay in here." Juan said.

Eleanor told him about the mattresses, almost directly across the hall. "Do you think it's safe enough to pull them in here?"

"I think we should. We may need to cover ourselves with them instead of sitting on them." Juan followed Eleanor out.

Within a few minutes they had two mattresses and were on their way to get another when the sounds of the storm became louder. Juan looked down the hallway to a back exit door. "That door can go at any time. Two is enough for now. It's not safe out here. It's not even that safe in the office, but don't tell Maria." Juan said.

"I won't. We should check on her shoulder and see if the children are still sleeping." Eleanor replied, as they changed course and went back inside the office.

The emergency shelter they found wasn't as far inland as Eleanor had hoped to be, but it was better than being stranded on the road. Outside she continued to hear the howling winds and the thunderous rain. She spoke to Juan about getting things ready tonight in case by morning they needed to move to higher ground.

Maria's shoulder was throbbing and painful to move. Juan, with Maria's directions, made a sling for it out of pillowcases and towels. Eleanor asked if she wanted Tylenol or Ibuprofen.

Chuckling, Maria told her Ibuprofen for now. "I can't believe how prepared you are. How long did it take you to pack?"

"Well, to tell the truth, I was a little apprehensive about being in a hurricane, so I packed for survival. I really thought I was bringing way too much stuff, but now I see I wasn't. If we had made it to a shelter, I wouldn't have needed all of these things. Eleanor explained.

"I'm glad you did and very glad you picked us up. This storm is ruthless." Juan interjected.

While Juan made Maria comfortable and checked on the children, Eleanor moved their things, the extra blankets and towels, to a counter. She finished and then assisted Juan moving the two desks close together and putting the mattresses under each desk.

All through the night their shelter continued to be bombed by mother nature as she pitched objects against the building. Eleanor continued to fight off the fear creeping up her spine. She heard more windows being shattered. The office door seemed to be beckoning to let the storm in. They heard what sounded like parts of the roof being ripped off. Maria cradled her two little ones on a mattress under the desk, and sheltered their ears from the sounds.

Darkness surrounded them as the hurricane attacked with the force of a mighty army. Eleanor knew God was protecting them. He provided this hotel and they were safe. The only light in the room came from flashes of lightening that escaped under the doors. Even in the dark room, she could tell Juan wasn't sleeping either. Her heart went out to this young couple.

The storm still showed no sign of relinquishing its power after several hours. The winds continued to scream like a small child who didn't get their way. A loud crash just outside the door jolted her from her thoughts. Maria and Juan covered the children with their bodies. Eleanor curled into a ball with her head under the desk. The wind mercilessly persisted to push against the door.

Juan spoke first. "I think part of the lobby roof blew off."

"I think you may be right. I am curious, but refuse to endanger our safety. All the hate and destruction in the world seems to be wrapped up in this one storm." Eleanor replied.

By early morning. the storm was lessening, but the waters were rising. Four inches of water were on the floor, and rising fast. It was time to move up a flight. Eleanor took Mateo while Maria helped Angelica. Juan followed with the backpacks and food. The first several rooms had glass covering the floor.

"I think we should go to the third floor. It may not be necessary, but I don't want to get in a dangerous situation and then struggle to get to safety. Eleanor, please help get everyone to the third floor. I'll leave the things here while I go back downstairs and get the blankets from the office before it's too late." Juan said.

The water had risen almost to Juan's waist. He quickly grabbed the blankets and made his way back up the stairs. He was glad Eleanor had thought to put the blankets on the shelf, as most of the furniture was already under water. Eleanor was near the second floor stairs waiting to help carry things.

"The water is rising fast down there. It's already to my waist. I don't think it will get to the second floor, but the decision to move up another floor may be for the best." Juan said in between heavy breaths.

Nodding, Eleanor added, "Thank you for your wisdom. God is taking care of us."

Maria suggested taking a room facing the main road so they could signal for help. Eleanor was impressed at this young mother. *She is really good in emergencies, thinking a plan through and knowing what is needed. She was extremely creative and resourceful making diapers out of pillow cases and towels. She found markers in the office and had me write HELP on a pillowcase, and then put it in the window.*

Eleanor learned that Juan had been a teacher in his home country, but was now stocking shelves at night. Maria was small in stature with long, dark hair, and the face of an angel. She was a nurse by profession, but working as a clerk in the grocery store. She said employees could take food that was damaged or at the expiration date. It wasn't always what they liked, but it helped keep food costs down. She explained they had good jobs back home, but their area had become a drug and war zone. They left everything to flee the violence. They learned to live on very little.

Eleanor prayed they would be found before the waters got any higher and supplies ran out. What she brought was not enough for five people, but with careful planning, it would last about three more days. Danger was still lurking like the enemy waiting to strike. She hung on to Psalm 23:4-5, one of God's many promises. *Even though I walk through the darkest valley, I will fear no evil, for you are with me; your rod and your staff, they comfort me. You prepare a table before me in the presence of my enemies. You anoint my head with oil; my cup overflows.*

Chapter 18
A New Family

The water was four feet deep on the first floor before it stopped rising. It was the fourth night at their emergency shelter. Food and water were getting low, but they could stretch it for a couple more days. It was a blessing in disguise to find a box of granola bars, several pre-packaged muffins, and some candy bars in the office. They kept constant watch for any signs of emergency vehicles, but so far, they were on their own. Juan had found several colorful pieces of material and hung them in every window, hoping someone would see them.

He was able to pry several windows open to let in a slight breeze. It was late afternoon on the fifth day when they heard a motor. Each of them raced to a window and started waving their arms and yelling. Eleanor went to the next room and waved a towel as hard as she could. *Please, Lord. They have to see us.*

An officer in the boat looked up and waved back. *He saw us. Thank you, God, for hearing my prayers.* Eleanor went back with the others as they gathered their belongings. She and Juan took their things to the second floor staircase. The water had gone down significantly, but it was still almost waist deep on the first floor. Maria's shoulder was still quite sore, so Eleanor carried Diego and Juan took Angelica.

"How many are there?" An officer asked as Juan handed Angelica to him.

"Five. Three adults, one with an injured shoulder, and two children." Juan then handed Diego to another officer waiting to help. Eleanor strapped on her back pack and held her camera bag on her head while Juan took the other items. After Maria was safe in the boat, officers assisted Eleanor and Juan.

As the boat pulled away they saw the destruction to their shelter. The lobby was gone, as were most of the windows on the first and second floors. It was a miracle they were alive. Eleanor's car had vanished. *It must be floating around somewhere. God provided shelter at just the right moment. He made sure I wasn't alone in the storm. He made me a vessel to help this family. He protected them. He protected me.*

Eleanor found out that she was much further south than she had planned on traveling. Somehow, she had missed her turn-off. She drove towards the worst of the storm instead of to safety. She knew, though, it was no mistake. God was in control and placed her at the right time to aid a young family.

They were taken to a shelter to stay until it was safe to travel. The shelter was crowded with people, put they had room for the group of five. The shelter provided food, water, blankets, and clothing. They had to remain at their temporary home for three days before boarding a bus back to a central hub, where people could get buses to their specific cities. When they arrived at the hub, Juan and Maria thanked Eleanor, and said goodbye, before turning to walk the four-miles home.

"Walk!" You can't walk four miles with two small children. Get on the bus." Eleanor was surprised they were going to walk.

"The buses are not meant for us. We don't want to wait and be told to walk. We will just walk." Juan said.

"The buses are meant for all of us. I will see to it they have room for you." Eleanor told them. "Trust me."

Juan and Maria could not believe the kindness of this woman. Neither of them had family to speak of. Their parents were dead and most of their siblings and cousins were part of the drug world or hiding from it. They had chosen to run. They ran quiet and fast, without looking back. It was a death sentence if caught.

The bus stopped in front of their apartment. Eleanor got off with them. She wanted to make sure they had a place to return to before leaving. The three stood and looked at the building with no roof and some outside walls gone. It wasn't totally destroyed, but still unlivable. Their two-room apartment was on the second floor. Eleanor watched the children while they surveyed the damage. After several minutes, they came down the steps and said most of their things were gone, either from the storm or from looters.

"That settles it. You're coming home with me. I'm not sure what my place is like, but it will be safer than here. I asked a policeman to call my pastor and he is on the way. Get everything you want, or worth keeping, and bring it down here. He should be here in about thirty minutes." Eleanor said.

Maria burst into tears and hugged Eleanor. "You are so kind, but we cannot, nor will not, be a burden to you or to anyone."

"A burden? You, my dear child, are not a burden. I have room and you need a home for your little ones. You also need to have that shoulder looked at."

"Eleanor," Juan said. "Maria is right. You don't owe us anything. We will be alright."

"Juan and Maria. Listen to me," Eleanor said, "You need a place to stay and I can use your help with repairs, which I pray won't be many. I have contacts that may help you find jobs. Again, I'm not sure what shape my place is in, but I am not leaving you here. Now, go and get your things."

The two looked at each other and like obedient children, did as Eleanor told them. It didn't take much time to sort through their meager belongings, but with the pastor's help the van was soon on the road loaded with people and things.

Pastor Tony told them that their area wasn't hit as hard as other parts of the island, but there was damage. "We were luckier than most. Being near a large city has helped get our power on sooner than those in the outlying areas. Don't get me wrong, some are still without power and you may be one of them." He let Eleanor know that most of the residents got out of town in time and were able to get to the shelters. A few stayed, but had a rough go of it. After listening to Juan as he relayed their experience, the pastor sent up a quick praise that God brought them together and protected them.

The streets were covered with tree limbs and other debris. Eleanor's yard was full of the same. They all noticed the roof was badly damaged and the garage was in bad shape. Juan, Pastor Tony, and Eleanor slowly walked to the condo door, while Maria waited in the van with her children. Seeing the outside damage caused them to pause at the door.

Hesitantly, Eleanor opened the door, fearing what she would find. For the most part, the hurricane shutters were still closed leaving little light in the condo. Thankful there was electricity, Eleanor turned on a few lights. She quickly noticed a thin layer of wet sand covering the floors along with glass from a few broken windows.

Juan and Pastor Tony took a walk around the condo to check for damages. Carefully the men moved branches and other debris so they could open the hurricane shutters. Pastor Tony gave the thumbs up that the condo's structure was good and they could stay there while the repairs and clean-up were done.

Eleanor was told the hurricane took a last minute and quick shift away from this side of the island. The winds were still of hurricane force, but the water surge was much less of an impact as what had been predicted. As the men walked around outside to note what repairs had to be done, Eleanor checked the inside. Some of the furniture was water damaged and would need to be replaced. She exhaled a long sigh, knowing how much work was ahead of her.

The Hurricane shutters opened, Eleanor looked out the large sliding glass doors and saw an endless view of sand, brush, and limbs. The patio needed to be shoveled from all the sand and her lattice walls were in a mangled heap half way to the beach. A pause of sadness and then a quick appreciation that the condo was livable with only minimal damage. She brought her thoughts back to the present and quickly went to the door to help her adopted family.

Juan brought in a sleeping Diego and a very tired Angelica. Eleanor motioned for him to follow her. He put the children on the bed while Eleanor got out a few light blankets and covered them. She then made Maria comfortable and instructed the men to bring everything into the dining room.

"Thank you, Pastor, for helping." Juan said.

"You're welcome. Please let us know how we can help. If you need to see a doctor Maria, I will get someone to take you. Please don't hesitate to call." Pastor Tony said. "That goes for you too, Eleanor. Call me. I still can't believe what you went through, but praise God you are all safe." He gave her a big hug and then said he needed to get back to help others.

Turning towards the couple, Eleanor said, "This is not the welcome I would have preferred, but it is a blessing that the walls are still standing and it's safe for us to stay here. I'm glad the children are settled and sleeping. What do you say we sit for a few minutes and have something to drink and then tackle getting the glass picked up? I'm afraid we need to wear shoes until we can make sure all the glass is gone."

Juan and Maria nodded.

"Please take a seat and I'll get the drinks." Eleanor said

Maria quickly spoke. "Please let me get the drinks. You have done too much already."

Eleanor smiled. "Why don't we both get the drinks."

They discussed what needed to be done and in what order. Eleanor then brought up sleeping arrangements. "Tonight, I want you and your little ones to take my room. It has the larger bed. I will take the guest room."

Juan immediately protested but Eleanor held her hand up and smiled. "This is just for tonight. Tomorrow, I propose we make the art studio your room and the children can have the guest room. We can move everything into my bedroom. What doesn't fit, I can put in the den or at the gallery."

"Eleanor. We cannot put you out like this. We will be fine in the guest bedroom with our children." Maria said.

"Maria is right," added Juan. "You must not go to so much trouble. We can all sleep in the same room. You don't need to move any of your things."

"I know I don't have to. I want to. Your children demand a lot and with taking care of them and recouping from the hurricane, you need a retreat, also." Eleanor explained.

They worked for the next hour sweeping up all the glass and most of the sand from the floors. Maria check the furniture for any glass fragments. It was time to sit and just relax. There was nothing more they needed to do tonight. Eleanor knew exhaustion would soon find them.

Juan opened the patio doors to let the breeze in, along with some sand. Eleanor looked at him and laughed. "Well, we can either be cool or sand free. I vote for cool."

After a few days, Juan and Maria were settled in their own room and beginning to feel at home. Juan moved Eleanor's studio out and the guest room furniture into the old studio. The insurance company had taken care of her claim quickly and within a few weeks, she had her money. It was time for her to replace the ruined furniture. She and Juan could now begin looking for a new car. After several hours she found a car similar to the one she had before. Juan continued to make repairs on the condo. The remnants of the hurricane were slowly fading.

Eleanor had a used crib and small bed delivered for the children. For their dressers, she took the two nightstands from her art table. The house was beginning to take shape. Juan and Maria had their own space and she was happy for them. It was different having others in the condo, after spending so much time alone. Different yes, but a good feeling.

Maria was washing the few clothes they had almost every day. Eleanor asked Juan to watch the children, because she wanted to give Maria a break and take her to lunch. He readily agreed, so the two women headed for what Maria thought was a break from the daily routine and lunch. Eleanor had more than lunch on her mind, though.

The mall wasn't crowded as they walked into one of the large stores. Eleanor took Maria to the children's department and promptly put clothes in a cart. Maria looked confused until Eleanor told her they were on a shopping trip. Despite objections from Maria, the clothes kept piling up in the cart. Maria was shaking her head the entire time, trying to get Eleanor to understand she could not accept all of this.

"A place to stay is gift enough. We are invading your home." Maria said.

"Nonsense. I can use the company and Juan is doing so many things that I just can't do. Think of your little ones." Eleanor replied. "Now, let's get you and Juan some clothes."

Maria began to protest, but Eleanor, the natural mom and teacher, held up her hand to signal there was no debate. "It's my payment for all the work you and Juan are doing around the house." Shopping done and packages locked in the trunk, they set out for a well-deserved lunch. It was a light-hearted drive back to the condo. Maria, for the first time in a year, was relaxed. She told Eleanor all about what life was like before they had to flee.

"It's been difficult to give up our careers that we worked so hard for. Juan has so much to offer children and he is forced to settle stocking shelves. He was a highly respected teacher back home and love by his students." Maria said.

Eleanor, with eyes on the road, replied, "I have some contacts at a few schools. I can't promise anything, but I'll make the calls. I don't want to get Juan's hopes up, so this is between us for now. Okay?"

"Okay." Maria couldn't help but smile inside and out; from head to toe.

For the next several weeks Juan painted some of the rooms, built a walkway to the stairs leading down to the beach, and put in an outdoor shower. While Juan was busy doing so much around the house, Maria was also busy with the two little ones, sewing, cleaning, and cooking. Eleanor stepped back and enjoyed watching the two of them; happy and busy.

Eleanor was also busy. She had spoken with two principals about Juan. The teaching staff was already in place, but they were willing to use him as a sub. If there was an opening at the last minute, they would call. She had better luck at the local health clinic. They were short two nurses and were excited to hear Maria had training. Until she could get licensed for the Virgin Islands, she couldn't work as a nurse. Except for administering medications, Maria would be allowed to do all other nursing duties. It would be a start for Maria, in the field she was trained for.

Maria, Juan, and Eleanor created a schedule for "children duties", to accommodate Maria's new job. Eleanor would watch Angelica and Diego when Juan was busy on a project. She told Maria to concentrate on work, her family, and relaxing, until she was used to her new job. Eleanor would take care of meals, though Maria was welcomed to cook and bake whenever she wanted. Life was beginning to have more purpose than just painting and volunteering. Eleanor was no longer alone. She had family.

The phone rang one afternoon. It was the high school principal. He had been given Eleanor's number from one of the principals she had contacted. He asked if Juan was there. Excited, but keeping her reserve, she called Juan to the phone. A yell went up from Juan as he swung Maria around. He had a teaching job. He would be teaching science at the high school. The principal would put in for a temporary certification until he could get all of his records. Juan would start in two weeks.

The three of them sat down and began to look over the work schedules. Angelica was now old enough to go into kindergarten or at least pre-kindergarten. Diego was another story. The question was daycare. Eleanor wanted to offer, but she would be starting back to work soon. She remembered the church was opening a daycare center and immediately called Pastor Tony to ask him when it would be opened.

He said they had finished preparing the three-room building next to the church and would be filling it with furniture and supplies next week. The staff was already to go. It would be open in the next three to four weeks. Eleanor was pleased there were still openings. She explained the situation and asked if there was anyone who would be willing to watch Diego until the day care would open. Pastor Tony said that Juanita would love to watch him for a few weeks. It was an answer to prayer.

One problem solved, now on to the next. Transportation for all three of them would have to be figured out. Maria could walk unless the weather was bad. Eleanor could take the bus to her school. She could walk, but with books and such to carry, it would be very tiring. Juan said that he should take the bus and let Eleanor have the car. The debate continued for some time before the phone rang again.

Eleanor paused the conversation and picked up the phone. "Hello."

"Mrs. Eleanor. This is Pastor Tony again. Juanita and I got to thinking about all of you going in different directions every day. How are you going to work out the transportation?"

"Well, as a matter of fact, we are in the middle of that discussion now. Any ideas?" Eleanor asked with a laugh.

"I do have an idea." He said.

Surprised, Eleanor responded, "You do?"

"Yes. I called a friend a few towns over that sells used cars. He has a car, but it's not in the best of shape. If Juan is willing, I and a few others in the church can help him fix it up." he said.

Eleanor's face lit up. She looked at Juan and Maria before responding. "How much?"

"He just wants it off his lot. He doesn't have time to fix it and needs the room for a new shipment of cars. The cost would be parts only." Pastor Tony explained.

"Wonderful news. Do you want to hold on while I ask them, or do you want me to call you back?" Eleanor asked.

"I'll hold. Ask them! Quick, ask them!" He seemed more excited than Eleanor.

Eleanor told Juan and Maria that Pastor Tony had a car and the only cost was fixing it up. A group of men from the church would help. Before she could finish Juan was yelling. "Yes! Yes! How soon can we get started on it?"

Eleanor went back to let Pastor Tony know, but he was already laughing. "Tell Juan I can pick him up tomorrow and we'll get to work on it. My friend will bring it to the mechanic's garage in the morning. Eleanor thanked him and hung up the phone. Prayers were answered before they were even spoken. *God definitely works in mysterious ways.*

Memories flooded Eleanor. She was once again preparing for an empty nest. She thought it would take a good six months before they could find a place of their own. Until then, she would enjoy their company and play Gramma to the little ones. She would miss them, but it was time they had their own place and she had hers. She was praying they would find something nice and affordable, but not too far away.

When she retired to her room that night, Eleanor allowed herself the memories of Logan and his selfless love for her and others. She thought about Ellery and how much she missed talking with her daughter; sharing even the smallest news. She missed David and his towering strength, so much like Logan and yet, so different. Then, there was Madison. The grandchild they had prayed for, cuddled, laughed and played with, as they watched her grow. Tears that hadn't fallen in a long time, began to fall. She was getting older. She had just celebrated her 66th birthday with friends. She had celebrated without Ellery, David, and Madison. In a way, she had celebrated alone.

The sun shone bright the next morning as Eleanor put away the memories. She wrote her daily letter to Ellery before looking out at the Caribbean Sea and praying for God to remind her that He is still in control and will continue to provide for her; even though she has lost so much.

Chapter 19
More Dead Ends

Madison was excited for her junior year. She worked out a plan to be home so she could help her mom and still take a few classes at the high school. Iris had talked to the principal making it possible for her to take drivers education during the summer. Having her license was making it easier for everyone. She could drive to school and take her mom to the rehab center on the days she had art and music lessons.

Iris would be leaving next month, so Madison was beginning to take over more and more responsibilities. She was an excellent student, but Ellery worried about her taking on too much. She wanted Madison to enjoy her high school years like other teenagers. She admired Madison, but would she be able to handle it once Iris returned home?

Finished with her homework, Madison went to find Iris to learn how to make mac-n-cheese. It was one of her mom's favorite dishes, but Madison couldn't seem to make it the way Iris did. She followed the recipe in the cookbook and it tasted okay, but not great. She was a little nervous to be left in charge, but she had no choice. She looked forward to spending the weekend with Angela. It would be her last sleepover for a while.

Each day Madison and Ellery spent some time searching for Eleanor. Iris helped when she could and many times offered a fresh perspective. They did a thorough search of Puerto Rico and the Dominican Republic, but found no leads. They went methodically through each city, checking names, hospitals, morgues, and health facilities. Ellery was wondering, after so much hope, that maybe they would never find her.

Today they were starting to search Saint Thomas. Each of them had their checklist and a city to comb through. It would take them several days, maybe a few weeks, to go through the island, city by city and town by town. Madison wished it was summer so she could spend more time searching. Her school studies took a lot of time, in addition to cooking, cleaning, and helping her mom.

Ellery was able to take care of herself and was beginning to do some cooking and other small tasks around the house.

She still needed help with her exercises twice a day. She knew the exercises were important for her recovery, but she dreaded doing them.

Iris was looking forward to being back home, but with mixed feelings, as she would miss Madison and Ellery. It was like having a much younger sister and niece. All of her nieces and nephews lived so far away so she only saw them on rare occasions. She did enjoy being closer to her sister and thanked God for all the time they had spent together in the last several months. She knew it was time to go and let the two of them settle into their new life together. But, she still worried it was too much for Madison to take on. She and Ellery had talked at length about this and ways to ease the responsibility that Madison believed she needed to take on.

It was late September and Madison was adjusting to her fall school schedule and home routines. Iris would be leaving in a few days. She would miss Iris and viewed her as a mentor; as an example of how Christ wants people to live their lives; giving unselfishly. Madison learned so much from her, but the lesson of how to live life as an example to others was the most impacting of all.

Iris had tears in her eyes. "I will miss you. You have become family to me. Thank you for coming into my life."

"No. Thank you." Ellery spoke as she hugged Iris. "You were there for my daughter when she so desperately needed someone. You were there for me and changed your life to help us. You have made the transition from hospital to home easy. You took the worry I had about Madison away so I could concentrate on getting better."

Madison was last to say goodbye. "I can't say thank you enough. I was so lost when Dad died and Mom was in the hospital. I was afraid of where I would live, when I would see her, and so many other things. You were there for me."

"I was simply used as God's vessel to provide to you what you couldn't provide for yourself at the time. I learned long ago in Peru that time is short and to survive, you must help each other."

"I know you must get on the road, but it's hard to let you go." Ellery said.

"I do need to get on the road. Oh, I hate goodbyes. Madison, keep me up to date on your search for your gramma. I'll keep searching also."

The three hugged each other tightly and said their goodbyes for the third time. Ellery and Madison watched as Iris drove down the street, arm out the window waving until she was out of sight. Side-by-side, they walked back into the house to a different day; a day without Iris.

Madison found some of her subjects hard, but she was determined to master them. She loved the days when she could take her mom to physical therapy and go to her art and music lessons. This was the time she was most at peace. Her art teacher was giving her more difficult assignments and even suggested she think about a career in art. It was the first time Madison thought about her future.

Searching took a pause, while Madison and Ellery maneuvered their new schedules. After a few weeks, they were able to return to the search. They decided to work on searching for Gramma before lunch each day and take a break on Saturday. Sunday afternoon seemed to be the best time to review their notes and make decisions on where to search next. Ellery made sure to send a weekly update to Iris.

Ellery wanted this Christmas to be special for Madison, so she booked a trip to Disney World. It was similar to the trip they had planned to Disneyland before Madison became ill and the accident. An additional surprise for Madison included a few days at Universal Studios and a day at Sea World. Madison was thrilled about their Christmas vacation, but a little sad that her dad wouldn't be part it. Still, she knew her mom needed this.

The trip proved to be therapy for both of them. Madison couldn't believe they were staying at one of the hotels inside the park. Ellery made more magic happen with a character breakfast and VIP treatment. Arrangements were also made to assist Ellery in getting around the parks. It had been a wonderful few days, but it was time to leave. On their way to the airport, Madison was lost in the pages of her book and missed the sign that said, Universal Park straight ahead. It wasn't until they pulled into the hotel circle that she looked up from the book she was reading. She looked at her mom, who was smiling, and asked, "Are we picking up more passengers?"

"No." Ellery answered her daughter. "We are getting out and checking in."

"Checking in? Checking in here?" Madison asked, still very confused.

"Surprise! We are spending three nights here at Universal Studios with a side trip to Sea World." Ellery spewed it all out like an overly filled tea kettle.

"What! Mom. This is so cool!" Madison squealed.

Madison couldn't wait to get into the park, but it didn't open for another thirty minutes. Ellery, noticing her daughter's anxiousness, suggested they get ready and then get something to drink while they waited for the park to open. They had two full days in the park, including express passes and Madison didn't want to waste one minute of it.

It was a great trip and what they needed. The time was spent enjoying the parks, weather, and each other. Now it was back into the routine. Madison was both a student and a caregiver. Even though Ellery could do many things for herself, she still lacked the stamina to do it all. Madison did most of the cooking while her mom helped with small things. Ellery was able to do some baking, which was something she had always enjoyed doing.

They had been back for a few weeks and the search for Eleanor had been moved to Saint John island. It was taking a little longer now with only two of them splitting the tasks. Still they had ruled out two of the larger cities and were now concentrating on the smaller towns and coastal areas. Madison knew there was only one island left to check in the U.S. Virgin Islands after Saint John and she was hoping to find Gramma on one of them.

Ellery came down with a bad viral infection and was told to stay in bed for two weeks. The doctors warned if she didn't, she may find herself back in the hospital. Knowing this could affect the progress she was making in therapy, she did as she was told. This meant more responsibility on Madison. Ellery asked the doctor's office to schedule an aide to come in for the two weeks. Once a day, a caregiver arrived and stayed for two hours allowing Madison to have a break.

Ellery, being on semi-bed rest allowed Madison to continue attending school, as she was only gone a few hours. Within a few weeks, Ellery was taken off bed rest and allowed to do small projects around the house. She was cautioned to take it easy or she may have a relapse. Madison was now able to spend a few more hours away from home.

Madison took over the search until her mom would be well enough to help her. It was close to Spring Break when she finished Saint John island. To her dismay, and Ellery's, there were no leads for this island. This was too often becoming the story. She had searched Cruz Bay and Coral Bay twice and even the Great Thatch island, just off the coast of St. John.

It was time to search the final island in this group before looking at the British Virgin Islands. *Gramma had to be somewhere in these waters. If not, I'm not sure where to look.* She took the list and began to search from the largest cities to smaller towns and coastal areas.

Spring Break arrived and Ellery was feeling much better. She and Madison decided to go to Chicago for a long weekend. Once again, she felt Madison needed a break from the everyday responsibilities. She promised Madison they would spend time each evening in Chicago searching for Gramma. It was a relaxing weekend for them. They enjoyed the indoor pool and Ellery splurged for them to spend a day at the spa, getting the works. Madison thoroughly enjoyed the spa day.

Every night, they continued trying to find Eleanor. They didn't find any leads in the major cities, so the concentration switched to the smaller towns. Back at home, they spent even more hours combing through the Internet. Once more their search came to a halt when Ellery was told she had to have one more surgery on her spine. They were relieved it could be done at the local hospital, which meant Madison could stay at home during the day and go to the Richardson's at night.

The surgery went well and with continued therapy, the doctors predicted Ellery would be able to move from walker to cane. They cautioned her that it would take time and not to try and rush the therapy. Ellery knew they meant well and were experts in their field, but they had no clue how discouraging to hear the news and yet be told to go slow. She looked at Madison, and for her daughter, she would follow the recommendation of her physical therapist.

It was late May and school would be out soon. Madison had gotten a lead on an Eleanor Morgan living in a coastal town in St. Croix. She was so excited, but kept it to herself. Her mom was doing well in therapy and she didn't want anything to jeopardize it. *Mom doesn't need any more stress or disappointments from dead end leads.*

Madison began to check various directories. One night she decided to spend time, going through each available school and church directory in St Croix. She was surprised how many churches had their members listed in addition to staff. She found an Eleanor Morgan as a part-time teacher at a small Christian school.

Gramma, a teacher? This can't be. I don't remember Gramma ever teaching school. Madison shoved her astonishment aside and continued to search. Eleanor Morgan's name came up again at a church in the same area. *This has to be more than a coincidence. This has to be Gramma. I can't tell Mom yet. I have to make sure.* Madison, again for a reason she couldn't explain, looked at the shops and restaurants in the nearby town. Maybe she would see her gramma in a picture. Optimism started creeping slowly in.

She had looked at over seventeen business websites, but no picture of a woman that could be Gramma. This seemed to be taking too much time and she thought about giving up the idea of looking on business websites. It was the end of May and she only had a week of school left. She needed to study for finals. This would have to wait until all her tests were done.

Exams done and school out for summer, Madison picked up where she left off, looking at more business websites. She told her mom to search some of the smaller towns on the other side of the island. She didn't tell her about her leads and felt somewhat guilty keeping it from her. *Mom has to heal. She can't go backwards and even though I should tell her, I can't risk this delaying her chance to use a cane.* She opened a website for an art gallery in a coastal town, when her mom called.

"Madison. It's time to leave for physical therapy."

This is such bad timing. "Okay Mom. I'll be right down." *This art work looks amazing.*

Two hours later they were back at home. Ellery was exhausted and sat on the sofa with her legs up. Madison turned on the television and got something for her to drink.

"I'll start dinner. Okay?" Madison said.

"How about we have pizza delivered?" Ellery suggested, knowing her daughter was probably as tired as she was.

Madison wasted no time in dialing the number. They both wanted to call it an early night. Ellery went to her room hoping to fall asleep, while Madison continued her search.

Okay. I want to see the pictures in this art gallery. She started to scroll through some of the paintings when one caught her eye. Looking at the painting made her feel like she was actually in the storm. She clicked on the picture to see a larger image and to read about the artist. The painting was done by – Eleanor Morgan! *This can't be. There has to be some mistake.* Madison scrolled down even further hoping to find a picture of the artist.

"Gramma!" Madison softly cried out. Tears forming as she stared at the picture of an older lady. "It's Gramma." She had found her. She didn't know what she should do and who, if anyone, she should tell before it was verified.

Chapter 20
Vacation Adventure

Madison decided to confide in Angela a few days later. She was spending the night so it gave Madison time to tell Angela what she found and talk over what to do next with someone she trusted.

"Maddie. You really think it's her? You think she's in St. Croix?"

"Yes. Look. Here's the picture of the artist Eleanor Morgan and here is an old picture I have of her." Madison showed Angela the two pictures.

"They do appear to be the same person. When are you going to tell your mom?"

"Not until I'm sure. I have a lot to check out first and I have to meet Gramma face-to-face before I tell my mom."

The girls were silent for a minute, each in their own thoughts, when all of a sudden, Angela blurts out, "Hey. My parents are booking a family trip to St. Thomas and St. Croix islands. What if I ask them if you can come with us?

Madison, turned to Angela. "I remember you talking about it, but I didn't know it was a definite trip for this summer. Are you sure you're going? Do you think they would let me come?"

Angela started laughing. "Which question do you want me to answer? My parents wouldn't say no to you coming. You and your mom are family."

"Great! When can we ask them?" Madison said.

Angela got very quiet before speaking. "Maddie. What about your mom? You'll have to tell her and who will take care of her while you're gone?"

Madison sat back against the bed. It was her turn to be quiet. She was so caught up in the idea of going to St. Croix that she forgot about her mom. "I just don't know. I'll work on that if you ask your parents if I can come."

"Will do. You also need to find your gramma's address and see how you can check it out when we get to the island. This won't be easy, you know." Angela added to the already many things Madison had to consider.

Madison spent the next week working out several plans. The Richardson's were more than happy for Madison to join them. Ellery also agreed it would be good for her to have some fun with a friend. All of them knew someone would have to come and stay with Ellery. It was time to ask Iris for another big favor.

Things were falling into place for the trip. Iris would stay with Ellery while Madison was gone. She said it was a good excuse to visit, not only with Ellery but spend time with her sister. Her nieces and nephews were coming into town one of those weeks and Iris was thrilled to be close enough to visit daily with them.

Madison found the address for an Eleanor Morgan. She hoped it was Gramma Eleanor Morgan. She couldn't think there would be more than one in St Croix. She was counting down the days and hours before she would board the plane and leave for the islands. The first stop would be St Thomas for five days and then a boat to St. Croix. Angela was getting all the details of where they were staying and what they would be doing. She hoped it would be close to the address she needed to check out.

Three days before Madison was to leave, Angela stopped by. The girls talked with Ellery for a few minutes and then excused themselves to the family room. Madison could tell Angela had news of where they were staying and possibly other details of the trip. Angela kept up the inconsequential chatter for several minutes.

"Okay. Angela. I can't take it anymore. Please tell me what you know." Madison said.

"Well, I have found out quite a bit. We are flying into St. Thomas for five days and four nights. We'll be staying at Harbour Point. My parents scheduled a few tours and then sightseeing on our own. I think we're going to a few islands also. Doesn't this sound like fun?" Angela was so excited and talking as if she had just downed a quadruple shot Mocha Latte.

"Angela. It all sounds great so far, but I am interested in St. Croix. Tell me about all the other stuff later." Madison was becoming exasperated.

"Oh. Sorry. Okay. We are taking a ferry from St. Thomas to Christiansted, St. Croix. It's about forty-three miles and will take ninety minutes. We're staying at a condo right on the beach near the boardwalk. It's right on the Caribbean Sea! Do you want to know what we'll be doing there?" Angela excitedly asked.

"Not now. I want to see how far Christiansted is from the address I have. If it's not too far, maybe we can schedule a tour near there or we can somehow ditch your parents long enough to check out the address." Madison needed to calm her friend down and get serious. She forgot that to Angela this is a vacation and she was looking for adventure, but to Madison it was a quest.

"Sorry, Maddie." Angela said trying to contain her excitement of the trip. "I'm not sure of all the places we're going, but I do know we're going to the Wildlife Refuge on the other side of the island one day and they mentioned spending a day at Cocoa Beach. They said the beach was only a short drive from the hotel. Either one of those places near where you think your gramma is?"

"Let's look at the map in my bedroom." Madison said as they ran up the stairs. The girls, still talking and laughing made their way to Madison's bedroom. Ellery just shook her head as they went by. She knew they were going to have a marvelous time in the Caribbean. Ellery was going to miss Madison, but was glad Iris would fill the void.

Opening up the map she saved on her computer, Madison found Christiansted. She opened her notes to see where the art gallery was and also the address she had for her gramma. Angela jumped as Madison let out a yell.

"It's close! It's close!" Madison was nearly jumping out of her chair. "Look Angela, I think it may only be a few miles or less from Cocoa Beach to the town and also to my gramma's!"

Angela couldn't believe it. All these years and Madison had found her. She prayed it was her gramma. The girls continued to talk and throw out ideas of how to get Madison to her gramma's house without Angela's parents knowing.

They came up with three different plans, depending on what they find when they get there. They also hoped Angela's parents would give them some time to explore on their own.

Changing the subject from planning to reality, Angela asked, "When and what do we tell my parents if you do find your gramma?"

"I guess that is something we need to tackle when, and only when, it happens." Madison said.

The day finally came to leave. The Richardson's arrived and loaded the luggage into the car. Kathy and Craig assured Ellery that Madison would be well taken care of, and that both girls would have a great time. Ellery nodded, knowing it was true and wishing someday, she and Madison could take such a trip.

Iris and Ellery said their goodbyes to Madison as she got into the car. Everyone had a different reason to be excited for this trip. Angela was going on an adventure, Ellery was happy to see her daughter take time to be a teenager, and Madison was on a mission to find her gramma and hopefully bring her home.

St. Thomas was beautiful and there was so much to do. Kathy noted Madison wasn't acting like the carefree girl she knew. She pushed it off as having a good time but worrying about her mom. She mentioned it to Craig and he said the same thing; she was just worried about her mom.

The water was warm and the sun hot. Angela and Madison were enjoying their last day on the beach before leaving for St. Croix in the morning. Madison finally broke the perfect silence. "What time do we leave tomorrow?"

"Maddie. Relax and enjoy the fact that my parents are letting us have a beach day without them hovering nearby. I think 9 or maybe 10." Angela said, a little disappointed that Madison wasn't enjoying the beach like she was.

"Sorry. Angela. I'm anxious and scared." Madison replied.

"I didn't think about you being scared. Hey. Let's go for a swim. That should get rid of the 'scaries' for a while." Angela suggested.

Madison smiled as she raced for the water. *Angela was right. It's a beautiful day to swim and lay on the beach without the others around.*

It was time to meet Angela's family for ice cream and shopping in the small coastal town. Later that night they took a dinner cruise around the island.

Lying in bed, Madison checked the time on her cell phone for the fifth time. Each time, it was only ten minutes later. Time was moving slower than a turtle crossing the road. Finally, Angela stirred and Madison jumped out of bed begging her to get up and get ready. Showered and dressed they set out to greet a new day.

Craig and Kathy bid the girls good morning and carried on the usual morning conversation. As soon as the entire group was ready, they made their way downstairs. Craig suggested they check the luggage at the ferry and then grab some breakfast. There was plenty of time before they set sail to St. Croix.

Kathy noticed that Madison seemed anxious and asked if she was nervous about the ferry ride over the open water. Madison insisted she was not, just excited about going to another island. Angela, Kathy thought, was acting like she had too much caffeine, although she knew that wasn't the case. *I wonder what the girls are up to.*

The ferry was finally on its way to St. Croix. Madison and Angela stood at the front, squinting to see a glimpse of the island. The girls pointed and started yelling at the others to look at the dolphins swimming alongside them. The water was like a window to the sea floor below. It water was so blue which made it difficult to see where the sky ended and the sea began.

Craig was enjoying the dolphins when Kathy interrupted. "Craig. I still think the girls are either hiding something or planning something. We are in a foreign country and I can't help but worry"

Laughing, Craig responded to his wife's intuition. "Kathy. Relax. They are normal teenage girls hoping shop, lay on the beach, and meet some teenage guys. It's as simple as that. Relax and enjoy the ride."

"I hope you're right." Kathy answered.

Madison pointed to the island ahead. St. Croix was in view and the shoreline was getting closer every minute. She couldn't wait to get into their room, unpack, and then have lunch. Lunch was where the schedule would be shared. She hoped that Angela would pay close attention and have some ideas about how they could get time alone. They were given a few hours in St. Thomas so she hoped the same would be true in St. Croix.

The condo was right on the beach, and quite large. It had four large bedrooms, each with its own bath, meaning the two boys got their own rooms and Angela would share a room with Madison. Kathy and Craig had a hard time containing all the excitement when the kids spotted the pool right on the beach, overlooking the water. Craig corralled everyone and led them to an area restaurant, hoping for some peace while they shoved food into their mouths.

The plan was finally presented. Today was roaming the streets of the city and tomorrow a cruise around the island and do some snorkeling. The final three days would be spent relaxing, with one day at Cocoa Beach, and the town. They would stay the final two days close to the condo enjoying the beach, pool, and walking to nearby restaurants and shops.

The schedule became a blur after she heard they would be going to Cocoa Beach. That was within walking distance to the address she held close to her heart. Tonight, she and Angela would finalize a way to be alone. Madison figured they could walk from the beach or the town to the address in a matter of ten minutes. She would worry later about what to tell the Richardson's if she actually found her gramma.

Today the group enjoyed the town of Christiansted and all the historical places. But in her head, Madison routed different ways to the address. She had memorized the map and most of the streets leading to the address. She seemed more relaxed today than she had been the entire trip and Kathy noticed.

"I think you were right. Teenage girls being teenage girls." Kathy said to her husband as they followed the kids down the street.

"The girls are easy to predict. It's all about boys and shopping." Craig laughed.

The second morning they all took a cruise around the island. Another warm day with calm seas. The island had several coastal towns and then long stretches of beach without any signs of civilization. The boat pulled in close to the shore for passengers to snorkel in the shallow waters.

After two hours of snorkeling, the boat set sail to finish the last leg of the trip. The captain announced they were passing Grande Beach. Madison went to the coastline side of the boat. Grande Beach was just before her gramma's place. She drank in all the houses along the way, wondering if any belonged to Gramma. *Could she be on the beach right now? Was she in one of those houses?* Madison couldn't keep the hope from rising in her chest that she would see her gramma very soon.

It was a bittersweet day as Eleanor helped Maria pack up the last of their things. They had found a small 2-bedroom house to rent close to where Juan was teaching. Saying goodbye was never easy for Eleanor, but she knew this special family wouldn't be far away. It was only a few miles on the other side of town. Today, she would be happy for their new beginning.

"Time to go Maria. Is this box everything?" Juan said.

"Yes. We're all done here. I'll get the children in the car. Maria answered.

Maria buckled the children in the car and set out to their new home. Juan and a few friends drove the truck and Eleanor brought up the rear of the moving caravan. The house was partially furnished and with the bedroom furniture she was giving them to take, little would have to be purchased. The house was in a good neighborhood of hard-working people. It was cozy, freshly painted, and had a fenced in back yard. Perfect for a family just starting out. A safe home.

It was late afternoon when Eleanor decided to leave. She had helped as much as she could. Most of the time was spent chasing after the two children, which left her exhausted. She hugged them all and told them to come for dinner soon. Putting the car in drive, she could feel every bone and muscle screaming her age. *I need a hot bath, a cool drink, a piece of chocolate cake, and my chair on the patio.* It wasn't long before Eleanor was sitting in her patio chair.

Juan had carefully helped Eleanor get all of her art supplies and furniture back in its proper place. She was anxious to get back to painting full time. Since she decided to retire and not teach this school year, she had plenty of time for her art and volunteering. The school was pleased that Eleanor offered to sub if available. She hadn't transferred the photos from her camera to her computer yet, and she wanted to get the photos of the hurricane printed and matted. She also had paintings in her head that needed to get on canvas.

Before the day got any warmer, she headed to the beach for a long, relaxing walk. She was alone again. This time it was different. There was no sorrow, only peace in knowing she helped make a difference in four lives. She looked out at the Caribbean Sea and smiled. Logan would have smiled too.

Chapter 21
Knock On the Door

The day had finally arrived. Madison was going to see if the address she had was the home of her gramma. She went over a million times of what she will say when her gramma opens the door, however none of them seem right. Mrs. Richardson had said they were planning on leaving around nine o'clock for the beach and then walking into the town for lunch. After lunch it hadn't been decided if they would return to the beach and then back to town to shop or shop first and then the beach. Mr. Richardson didn't know why they couldn't just go with the flow.

Kathy thought the beach and town were quaint and would make for a great day. Madison and Angela were acting like detectives, looking at all the street signs, and familiarizing themselves with all the shops. They parked near the beach, quickly gathered their things, and then went to claim a spot in the sand. Angela's brothers made straight for the water, while her parents spread out the blankets and cooler.

Angela told her parents that she and Madison were going to walk along the water and would check in with them if they decided to go for a swim. Craig told them to have a good walk and they would either be here on the beach or in the water with her brothers. Angela waved as she and Madison started walking towards where they thought Eleanor lived. They had decided not to go too far right now, but later, they would take a longer walk. A walk to Gramma's door.

Eleanor walked along the water's edge enjoying the day. She usually walked towards Grande Beach, but today, she walked towards Cocoa Beach. A change in scenery is what she wanted, although most would say, the beach and water are the same either way you go. Eleanor begged to disagree. She noticed the small things along her walks that were unique. She observed the location of the sun which allowed shadows to be cast in various patterns, and the games the waves played together, depending on the force and direction of the wind, as they crashed unto the shore.

The walk gave new life to her tired body. *Angelica and Diego really tired me out yesterday. I'm not that old, but I am definitely out of practice. God, bless these two little ones and support Juan and Maria. Thank you, Lord, for the time I spent with them.* Her body told her it was time to turn around and head back to her waiting chair. Eleanor talked to herself the rest of the way back.

They found a great outdoor café in town and ordered lunch. All of them were starved for a good burger and fries. Kathy noted that it wasn't really unbearably hot with the breeze coming off the water. They talked and laughed for about an hour before Craig asked what was next on the agenda; beach or shopping. The boys wanted the beach and the girls wanted shopping. It was decided. Craig would return to the beach with the boys, which he didn't mind at all, and the girls would enjoy a few hours in town.

"I was thinking that maybe you girls would like some time to shop on your own. Would that be okay? I'm thinking we have different shops we want to look at." Kathy said.

"Oh, can we Mom?" Angela asked.

Kathy nodded before answering. "Yes. Do you want to meet back here in a few hours or the beach?"

"The beach." They both said.

Kathy laughed and reminded them to check in every hour. She told them she would see them at the beach in a few hours.

Angela and Madison looked at each other in disbelief. This had been easier than all the plans they worked out. The girls got out the map and headed to the address Madison had protected during the trip, even though it was forever etched in her heart. They started down the street that led them out of town. Continuing to follow the map, they hoped it was correct. It was only four blocks from the restaurant to the row of condos.

Madison stopped so suddenly that Angela ran into her. "Is this the place?" Angela asked.

"I think so. According to the address it should be the fourth door." Madison said, but didn't move.

"So, are you going to knock on the door or not?" Angela was anxious for Madison.

"I'm really nervous, but I have to. Where do you want to wait for me?" Madison asked.

"I'll go down to the beach and walk around. Don't forget, we have less than two hours. Maybe you should set the alarm on your phone for fifteen minutes before time is up. I'll set mine. I'll head back up here if I don't see you on the beach." Angela said as she hugged Madison for good luck.

Madison stood there a few minutes, alone. She began to walk slowly to the fourth condo, then stopping, before taking a few more steps and stopping, again. Madison thought she was doing more stopping than actively moving forward. She walked down the paved path to the door and gently knocked. Her heart racing. There was no answer. She knocked again, harder. *What if no one answers?* Her palms were sweaty, heart pounding as if it wanted to jump out of her body, and her mouth was dryer than dirt in a drought. *Maybe this is the wrong door.*

Hearing footsteps, Madison focused on the sound. She couldn't tell if the steps were coming closer to the door, but then the footsteps stopped. She needed more time before confronting the owner of the home, possibly her gramma. *Should I really be here? I wish Mom was here with me. I'll go and come back later if there's time. Too late.*

The door opened slowly and an older woman stood there. Madison's heart stopped along with any ability to breathe. It was Gramma. *What do I say? I have to keep my emotions in control. Please God. Help me."*

The bright afternoon sun caused Eleanor to take a moment to focus her eyes on the young woman standing at her door. "Hello. I apologize, my eyes need a second to focus in this light."

"Take your time." Madison's voice was shaky.

I know that voice. Am I hallucinating? "Please. Come in." Eleanor's eyes, now able to focus, saw a young Ellery standing there. She stumbled back holding onto the wall for balance. Crying out – "Who are you?"

Madison stepped inside the door and quickly reached out to support her gramma. Eleanor's one hand went to her heart and the other to cover her mouth. *Could it be? Could this be Madison?* As much as Madison tried to hang on to her emotions, they let loose. Tears flowing freely and hands trembling, as she continued to support her gramma, she spoke between sobs.

"It's me, Gramma. It's Madison."

Eleanor's legs were giving way, but Madison held her tight. Loud sobs exploded from Eleanor. Madison continued to embrace her gramma as her body shook with loud sobs, as well. She kept saying, "I'm sorry. I'm so, so sorry."

She finally released Madison enough to look at her. "Welcome back Madison. Is your mom and dad with you?"

"No. I'm sorry she's not. She doesn't even know I've found you." Madison said.

"Please. Please. I need to sit down. I'm still quite shaky and in disbelief." Eleanor said.

"I have so much to tell you Gramma, and to ask your forgiveness." Madison was finally able to get the words out.

The two went into the family room and sat on the couch. Eleanor had prayed for this miracle, but so many years had passed and she had been pig-headed about reaching out, she thought God had a different plan. A horrible thought went through her mind – *is she here to tell me she hates me? Did she find me to continue the torment?*

Madison asked her gramma to let her tell the entire story before asking any questions. "I became jealous and joined a chat room, where they convinced me to do something about it. It made sense to me, and I started listening to them instead of the inner voice that told me otherwise. They helped me plan it all out. After Grampa died, I thought you were going to stay away, but you started coming back into the picture and, my so-called friends, convinced me you would be moving in and taking all my parent's attention and time. They told me how to get rid of you for good."

She took a long breath. Even though she was able to talk, the tears continued to spill out. Madison went on to tell her gramma about how she felt later. "I was too stubborn to say anything. But then, I got very sick with meningitis. I spent a long time in the hospital. During my stay, God spoke to my heart and I repented. I found the courage to confess it all to my parents. They were angry, but forgave me and helped me search for you. Mom had already been searching for you, without telling us. Gramma. I am sorry. I have been trying to find you for the last three years to ask your forgiveness. Will you forgive me?" There was a pleading in her eyes.

Eleanor took her granddaughter's face in her hands. "Yes. My dear, dear Madison. Yes, I forgive you. I searched my heart for so long to find an answer to why you hated me. I'm glad I now know the truth."

After a few moments of silence, Eleanor said, "Is it time for me to ask questions?"

"Yes." Madison looked at the time and saw she still had thirty minutes.

Eleanor's first question was a practical one. "Do your parents know you are here?"

Madison took a deep breath. No. Mom is at home, still searching. There was an accident in February. Mom was critically injured and recovery has been long. She was in a wheelchair, but is now using a walker. She's working hard to start using a cane." Madison's voice softened. "Dad …uh, …dad was killed instantly."

"And I wasn't there. Oh Madison. I'm so sorry I wasn't there. My pride kept me from my daughter when she needed me most. My pride kept me from being there when you needed me. I loved your father, even with the problems and separation. I was so caught up in my own selfish hurt, that I didn't make any attempt to contact you." Eleanor responded.

Madison told her about Iris and how she helped them get through some tough times, before Eleanor asked, "How did you finally find me?" Eleanor asked.

She told her how they searched all fifty states. She explained that her parents went to speak to the neighbors and the family that bought her house. Then the accident happened and they stopped searching for a long time. Iris found out from the realty company that you moved to the Virgin Islands, which really helped get the search going down the right path

"I was down to the last island and found your name listed. Searching further, I saw your name as a teacher and a member of a church here. I still wasn't sure and didn't want to give Mom false hopes, so I started looking through the business websites, hoping to see you in a picture. I was taken in by a painting on an art gallery website. When I scrolled down, the artist was you; it had your picture. This is when I knew I had found you." Madison let out a long sigh. She had finished her story.

Eleanor shed tears for David, for Ellery, and for Madison. She couldn't believe all of this had happened since she left. She felt a pang of guilt for not being stronger and staying put. "I'm so sorry for running away. I should have been there for you and your mom, instead of you bearing all of this alone."

"No Gramma. You didn't have a choice. Dad and I gave you no hope. Although, I really didn't think you would leave." Madison quickly said.

Eleanor couldn't help but see the pain and regret in her granddaughter's face. She wanted to keep Madison there. She wanted to talk to Ellery. First, she needed to know how Madison got to the island. "Now, who are you here with?"

Madison explained that she was here with her best friend's family. Only her best friend knows what she is doing.

"Where is your friend and her family now? Do they have any idea where you are?" Eleanor wanted to know.

"Angela is down on the beach. I have ten minutes before I'm to meet her and walk back to Cocoa Beach. That's where her parents are."

"I'm relieved to know that you are here with responsible adults and they aren't running around searching for you or reporting you missing to the police. That would be very unfortunate for both of us." Eleanor said. "So, you have done a lot of planning. How are you planning on telling Angela's parents, and your mom, what you've been up to?"

"That is the one part of the plan Angela and I haven't figured out yet. Any ideas?"

"Yes. You need to return to Cocoa Beach – on time. You and Angela need to let her parents know tonight about this escapade you pulled. Inform them that I will meet them tomorrow morning around 9 a.m. to discuss where we go from here. When do you plan on calling your mom?"

"I can handle telling the Richardson's, but I don't want to tell my mom all of this on the phone. I want to wait until I get back, but I need the Richardson's and you to agree." Madison said.

"I tend to agree that your mom must be told in person and not over the phone. I will talk to the Richardson's tomorrow about that, as well. Tell them to wait on calling your mom until I speak with them in the morning. When do you fly home and what airline?" Eleanor was thinking about next steps.

She gave Madison her phone number and got the address of where she was staying. Eleanor held Madison's hands as she prayed that her granddaughter would have the words to say when telling the Richardson's and that this couple would have a listening and compassionate heart. She prayed that the two girls would get back to Cocoa Beach safely. Finally, she thanked God that a fractured relationship was being repaired.

Madison met Angela on the beach with several minutes to spare. She looked up at the condo and saw her gramma on the patio. They waved and then the girls turned and walked down the coast. Angela asked a million questions all within a minute. Out of breath, she waited for Madison to fill her in as they walked back to Cocoa Beach.

Later that night, while the boys were watching a movie, Madison and Angela went outside to the deck, where Craig and Kathy were sitting. They moved their chairs closer to them. Kathy, aware that the girls wanted to talk, thought they were going to ask to do more shopping. She had been surprised they returned to the beach without buying anything.

"Mr. and Mrs. Richardson?" Madison said.

"Yes, Madison." Kathy answered.

"I have something to talk to you about. Angela already knows, but I did this on my own and asked her to come with me."

Craig was now paying attention. "Are you in trouble? Did something happen in town?"

"No. Nothing like that. You know my mom and I have been searching for my gramma for a long time now. Well, last month I found an Eleanor Morgan living here in St. Croix. Later I found a picture of an Eleanor Morgan and she looked just like my gramma." Their jaws dropped in disbelief as they leaned forward, listening intently, as Madison continue.

"When I told Angela, she asked me to come along and maybe I could contact this woman to see if she was indeed my gramma." Kathy started to speak but Craig took his wife's hand and squeezed it; a signal to wait. "The address was in the town where we ate today. Instead of shopping, Angela and I walked to the house. She stayed on the beach, just outside the condo, while I went to see if it was my gramma."

"And?" Craig urging her to continue.

"And, it was. My gramma is here and I spoke with her and also asked her for forgiveness. She wants to speak with you tomorrow morning."

"Is this really true? You found your gramma? We have to call your mom!" Kathy blurted out.

"No! Please don't call my mom! I don't want to tell her this over the phone. I need to be with her when she hears the news." Madison pleaded.

Craig and Kathy were silent for a moment before answering. "Kathy, I agree with Madison. We need to wait and let Madison tell Ellery when she gets home. It's only a few days." Craig reassured Madison that no one would tell Ellery. "Where are we meeting your gramma and what time?"

"She will be here at 9 a.m. Is that okay?" Madison asked.

"That's fine. The boys can play on the beach or in the pool while we talk." Craig looked at Kathy, who was still trying to process everything that had been said.

"That sounds good to me." Kathy replied.

Later that night Kathy looked at Craig. "Teenage boys, huh? Shopping, huh?"

Craig laughed and kissed his wife goodnight.

Chapter 22
A Strange Souvenir

"Mrs. Richardson?" Eleanor asked as the door opened.

"Yes. It's so good to see you again, Mrs. Morgan. Please come in." Kathy opened the door wide to allow Eleanor to step inside before giving her a hug. "This was a surprise to us last night and I'm sure to you also."

"It was a blessed surprise and an answer to many years of prayers." Eleanor said.

Kathy showed Eleanor to the deck where Craig and the two girls were sitting. Craig hugged Eleanor and welcomed her. He invited her to sit down and explained that if he wasn't looking at her it was because he was watching their two sons on the beach. Eleanor smiled and said she understood completely.

Kathy brought out coffee, juice and a blueberry coffee cake before they got started. "Mrs. Morgan –"

"Eleanor, please."

"Eleanor. Madison told us the whole story of how she and Angela left town to find your place. I must say, I wondered why two teenage girls came back with no packages. But, the bigger question is, Ellery. She needs to know, but Madison, and with a good reason, doesn't want us to call her. Do you agree?"

"I do. For more reasons than you or even Madison are aware of." Eleanor responded.

The group looked confused as Eleanor continued. "This was a shock, and very emotional to me, and Madison was there in person. Don't get me wrong, it was a beautiful shock and one I've been waiting for. Can you imagine Ellery getting a phone call from Madison telling her she not only found me, but saw and talked to me? She would be happy, yes, but she would also be hurt, frustrated, and wishing she was here." Eleanor paused so the group could process what she had just said.

"I think Gramma has a point. I know I would also be angry. There would be no one to hug and rejoice with. I do think we need to make sure Iris stays there while Mom is told. She helped in the search and has been a constant support for Mom." Madison added.

"So, you're saying that we need to finish our vacation knowing this truth and not let her know?" Craig asked.

"That's exactly what I'm saying. It's like keeping a wonderful surprise until it's time for the person to unwrap it." Eleanor hoped her example made sense to them.

"It will be a wonderful surprise and Madison can even have her gramma on Zoom right after Ellery is told." Kathy thought her idea brilliant. Everyone was nodding and starting to talk about ideas of how the Zoom would go.

Eleanor took a sip of her coffee and raised her hand slightly. She didn't want them getting too excited in the planning process before she proposed what she wanted to do. "If I could, and I thought about this all night and even this morning. I have a proposal that I'm hoping will meet everyone's approval."

Everyone looked at Eleanor, waiting to hear more.

"I would like to fly back with you. I don't want you or even Madison telling Ellery without me being there to hold her."

Kathy let out a loud! "Yes! That would be the best medicine for Ellery."

Madison jumped up and ran to her gramma. "Oh, Gramma. Would you? I mean, could you? Is it possible to get a ticket in just a few days? I would love you come back with me."

Eleanor laughed at the barrage of questions from her granddaughter.

"Well, it sounds like everyone approves, so I'll get busy and call the airlines to see if there are any seats available." Craig said.

"Too late, Craig." Eleanor said. "I called last night and I have a ticket, on what I'm hoping, is the same flight you are all on."

Everyone cheered and Kathy said that a celebration dinner was in order. She asked Eleanor for suggestions on where to dine. It was decided to all meet at The Boathouse around 6 p.m. for a time of rejoicing and celebrating.

Eleanor told Madison to spend the last two days enjoying the beach, shopping, and hanging with her friend. She assured her there would be many days ahead for them to spend together.

Today was the last day in St. Croix for the Richardson's and Madison. As promised, it was a day on the beach with Kathy taking the girls to town for some last minute shopping. The girls went from shop to shop and purchased several beachy items. They had a quick lunch and then headed back for some beach time.

Eleanor also had much to do. The beach beckoned her every time she looked out, and even though tempted, she resisted, and continued to clean and pack. She called

Charlotte to ask if she was available to get her mail and water her plants while she was away. She wasn't sure if she was packing too much or not enough. She had to make sure she had room for her camera and laptop. Pictures were in order and lots of them. Eleanor smiled as she packed several of the daily letters she had written to Ellery; glad that she had taken time to capture each day they had been apart.

She told the Richardson's that she would meet them at the airport even though they offered her to have the shuttle pick her up. She politely declined, saying she wanted her car there for transportation when she returned. Time was close to seeing her Ellery again, if all went as planned.

Was God really beginning to heal my fractured heart and life? Logan would be so pleased. I have been blessed with so many friends and island family, but my heart has still been alone. I'm praying that this is the beginning to that end.

It was time to leave for the airport. Butterflies hadn't been felt in her stomach for many years, but today, they had all come out of their cocoons and were fluttering around inside. At the airport she parked her car in the long-term lot and made her way to the terminal. She was relieved to see everyone full of smiles and excitement.

Kathy was worried that Eleanor was sitting by herself. Eleanor quickly assured them, she had done quite a lot of traveling in the past few years and it didn't bother her at all.

She welcomed the time alone reminisce and to think about seeing her Ellery again.

After the short layover, Madison was back in the air and headed for home. In a few hours she would see her mom. She couldn't wait to show what else she brought back from the islands. Kathy asked Iris to stay a day longer, as Madison wanted to see her. Iris wanted to see Madison, too and hear all about her adventures.

The plan was to drop Eleanor off at the corner and then swing around the block and park in the driveway. This would block the view to the end of the street. It should work. To Ellery it was just another return from a vacation.

Madison got out and ran to the door hugging her mom and Iris, while Craig got all of her luggage inside. Kathy and Angela came in long enough to say hello and that they had a wonderful time. Madison listened for a text from Gramma, signaling she was at the front door.

"Mom. I brought back the most unique souvenir for you. You won't even be able to guess what it is." Madison said with a smile that covered her whole body.

"Oh. Really? Does Iris know what the souvenir is? Ellery asked.

"No. Madison hasn't told me a thing. I wish she had because who knows what it might be. I'm as curious as you are." Iris stated.

"Okay. Promise you will sit down and close your eyes. No peeking. I left it on the front porch." Madison said.

"I hope it's not a snake or some type of exotic insect." Iris laughingly said.

Madison opened the door and motioned for her gramma to come in quietly. "No, it's not a snake or a bug. But thanks for the suggestion. I can do that next time."

Eleanor could hardly move as she saw Ellery on the sofa, and the walker next to her. She slowly got in front of her daughter and waited for Madison to tell them to open their eyes.

"Hi, honey. I'm your souvenir." Eleanor reached for Ellery to help her stand.

They stood holding each other for a long time. No words needed. The love was never lost.

Iris and Madison looked on, both emotional as well. After they released each other, Eleanor touched Ellery's face and smiled. The two women sat next to each other on the sofa before Eleanor spoke.

"Ellery. My dear, dear Ellery. I'm so sorry and ashamed for running away like I did. For not being patient. For only thinking of myself at the time. I believed, at the time, I was the only one hurting. I had just lost your dad and then you. I was hurt and angry. I have been a stubborn old lady for too many years. Please forgive me."

Ellery was taken aback by her mother's statement. "Mom. I never thought of you running away, but only as a way for you to survive. I'm sorry for not giving you a chance to explain your side, for turning my back on you when you needed me most. Dad had just died and then you had to bury us also. Please. Forgive me."

Madison smiled, but knew she was the cause of all of this heartbreak and division. Eleanor saw Madison's face and motioned her to come over. Gently she told Madison that even though her lies started all of this, each of them had a responsibility in the destruction. "All of us have asked for forgiveness and all of us have been forgiven. Now is the time to move forward; to repair the brokenness and loneliness we have all endured.

Ellery was ready to hear the story of how Madison found her mom and how she and the Richardson's kept it a secret. Iris quickly held up her hand and told them to wait before starting while she went to get everyone a cold drink and some cake. Her reasoning was that the body just expelled an enormous amount of energy and needed to be replenished. True or not, she said it was a good excuse for cake.

Madison explained, that towards the end of May, she thought she had found Gramma, but wasn't sure. When Angela invited her to go to with them on vacation, she knew it was a chance to see if what she found was true. She continued to search for an address and found one that matched the name.

"I couldn't believe that we were going to be so close. Mrs. Richardson planned one day at the beach and town where gramma lived. Angela and I waited until we had been given shopping time alone and then walked to Gramma's condo. Mr. and Mrs. Richardson didn't know anything until after I found Gramma."

She continued to tell her mom about the meeting with Gramma, how she broke the news to the Richardson's, and Gramma flying home with them.

The night was spent catching up. Eleanor learned more about Madison's illness and confession, about David's change of heart, the accident, and the search. She also learned about the selflessness of Iris. Ellery learned her mom had taken up painting again, added photography, taught for a few years, and took a long trip to Alaska and the Canadian Rockies. She also heard about the hurricane and the family that lived with her for a time.

It was early morning before they all went to sleep. It was a peaceful and satisfied sleep that the three had been waiting many years for. Iris was leaving in the morning, but said she would come back before Eleanor left. Eleanor thanked Iris for being the angel-on-earth God sent at just the right time.

Chapter 23
Home

At breakfast, Eleanor announced that she had a proposal. The three were all ears as she spoke. "I would like you and Madison to come live in St. Croix with me. Now, before you say, Madison's life is here or we have a house to sell and so forth, hear me out."

The three looked at each other confused, but Eleanor trudged on. "There is a wonderful high school in the area, or Madison can continue with homeschooling. If this isn't something you want to even consider, I understand. But, the offer is good now and after you graduate. The condo next to me went up for sale the day we left. I contacted my realtor and she put an offer on it for me, contingent on a final decision in five days."

Mouths still open and eyes wide, Madison was the first to speak. "Gramma. It would be hard to leave everything I know and love here. Angela is really my only close friend, but if Mom wants to, I'll think about it."

Iris looked at Ellery wondering what she was thinking. Ellery didn't leave her wondering for long. "Mom. This is an offer hard to pass up, but what about this house? It won't sell in five days, maybe not even in five months. What about all this furniture and years of, well, junk?"

Looking at Eleanor, Iris decided to butt in. "Ellery. You have way too much, as you say, junk. It's time to purge. The three of you have a chance to start over. To start new. Get rid of everything that you absolutely do not need or want. It's a beautiful offer. However, this is me, Iris, speaking. There. I've said my peace. And, by the way, I'm staying another night or until the decision is made."

Eleanor decided to speak from her heart. "We have been separated for too many years. This family was fractured and now we have an opportunity not only to put it back together, but seal all the cracks. Maybe I should offer to move back here, but my heart and home is now in St. Croix. However, if it will seal those cracks, I am willing to sell everything and move."

"Mom. This house and city have good memories, but also the constant reminder of David. I want to spend a few days to think and pray about it, and also to give Madison time to do the same. My heart longs to be with you. I don't want to say goodbye again." Ellery said.

"That sounds wise and practical, which you have always been. You are a planner and this move would put your planning to a test. How about we all get ready and go to the mall. I have missed eating at the food court." They all laughed when Eleanor mentioned the food court.

Ellery asked everyone to come sit at the table. She and Madison had made a decision about moving. Eleanor sat still with her hands folded and Iris sat fidgeting waiting for Ellery to speak.

"Madison and I have decided to move to St. Croix." Ellery announced.

Eleanor squeezed Madison's hand while sending a thank you up to God. She was happy, but knew a lot of work was ahead of them. Iris started clapping and giving air high-fives to everyone.

"I will call Amaya and let her know to put sold on the condo. I will also find out if they are leaving any of the furniture. Next, we have to list this house and you, Ellery, need to make a list of what is going and what is staying."

Iris interrupted their planning talk. "Before all of you get busy on the immense task ahead, I have something to say. As you know, my brother-in-law died last year leaving my sister alone. Her children are scattered around the country and aren't able to help her much. We have talked about moving in together, but neither of us has a house that gives us enough space for all our combined special 'junk' and space when her children come to visit."

"Are you wanting to move to St. Croix, too?" Madison asked.

"Heavens no. Though, I plan to come visit. What I am saying, or rather asking, is – would you consider selling this house to my sister and I?" Iris finally got the words out.

"Really?" Ellery asked, not quite believing what she just heard.

"Of course, really." Iris quipped. "I called my sister right after Eleanor said she wanted all of you to move to St. Croix. She likes the idea. It would let her stay in the area where she raised her family and attend the same church. She's always been a home-body. It would let us each have our own bedroom and bath plus an extra room to use as a personal retreat. The family room would give visitors a place to stay."

Ellery continued to look at Iris, not knowing what to say. Madison thought it was a good idea and Eleanor said sold. Iris on the other hand was waiting for Ellery to speak; in which she finally did. "I couldn't think of a better person to have my house. I would love to sell it to you. "

"Lunch on me. How does pizza sound? We'll have it delivered so we can make lists, all kinds of lists while we eat." Eleanor announced.

"You are a lady after my own heart. Eat while you work." Iris said.

Things moved quickly. In a few short weeks, the house had been sold and items shipped. There had been many farewell parties. The church gave Ellery and Madison a beautiful send off and a love offering to help with expenses. Other people gave farewell parties and gifts, including David's former office and their neighborhood.

The Richardson's, Iris, and her sister were the last to say goodbye. The Richardson's drove them to the airport. Angela was in tears saying goodbye to her longest and dearest friend. Senior year wouldn't be the same without Madison.

Kathy hugged Ellery goodbye and said they would stay in touch and definitely make St. Croix a vacation destination every few years. Ellery promised to return for visits, as well. With a set of final hugs, goodbyes, and tears, the three disappeared into the sea of passengers.

It was a good flight with no delays. St Croix welcomed them with a beautiful sunny day. They got into Eleanor's car and headed towards the condo. Amaya stood there with the keys as they pulled into Ellery's new home. Ellery had the same response Eleanor had when she first saw the place years ago. "It's beautiful."

"Wait until you see the beach, Mom." Madison yelled as she ran to the door.

"Eleanor, this must be your daughter and granddaughter. Welcome to St. Croix, Ellery and Madison." Amaya shook their hands and gave Ellery the keys. "I'm not going to stay, as you have an excellent guide right here. Please call if you need anything."

Amaya hugged Eleanor. "It seems all is put back together now, like finding the missing puzzle piece."

Eleanor thanked Amaya. Indeed, the puzzle was now complete.

Madison graduated at the end of the year and applied to the local college to study art and music. She had become fluent in Spanish in just a short time.

Ellery was now using a cane and teaching part-time at the Christian school. She spent hours reading the letters her mom wrote to her but never sent.

Eleanor spent her days painting, photographing, and walking on the beach. She was content, knowing her family was next door and that the fractured lives they had all experienced were completely and wholly mended.

The fractures repaired and the loneliness gone.

Together at last.

About the Author

Loraine Clinton Phillips is a retired educator who tried to instill in her students a love of learning through books, projects, and travel. Loraine has always had a passion to write, from high school poetry and journals to writing novels and children's picture books. This is her first novel after writing and illustrating seven children's books.

She makes her home in Lake Odessa, Michigan, where her husband of 48 years encourages her creative talents. Together they have a beautiful daughter, wonderful son-in-law, and four amazing grandchildren, whom she loves to spend time with. Some of her other interests include photography, quilt making, sewing, knitting, and crocheting.

Loraine has a BA in Psychology and Speech/Theater, MS in Instruction Design for Online Learning, and EdS in Leadership and Administration.